Nobody's

Perfect

Pat Ballard

Pearlsong Press
Nashville, TN

Pearlsong Press
P.O. Box 58065
Nashville, TN 37205
www.pearlsong.com

ISBN: 0-9713247-9-4
This ebook contains the text of the 2001 softcover edition published by Writers Club Press, an imprint of iUniverse.com, with minor revisions.

Library of Congress Control Number: 2004104467

Other books by Pat Ballard available from Pearlsong Press:

A Worthy Heir
Dangerous Curves Ahead: Short Stories
His Brother's Child
Wanted: One Groom

To Joe — my husband —
thanks for giving me the time to write.

To Eric — my son —
my perfect model for Jake.

To Ellen — my sister —
a fantastic copy editor!
Thanks for making me look good.

Chapter 1

Nella pulled the door closed behind her, stopping on the patio long enough to replace a cushion that had blown from a lounge chair before heading down the long flight of steps that led from the back patio of her home down to the sandy beach. As soon as her feet touched the sand, she turned and looked back at the house that had been her home all of her life.

Even though the bricks on the house were fading from the salty breezes that constantly blew against them, and the occasional harsh storms that came ashore, her father had always kept the shutters and trim work painted a startling white. Tears blurred her vision as she turned and continued down the beach toward the water. She could do her best thinking just sitting and listening to the waves lap against the shore.

She had only taken a few steps when she heard a child crying. Looking around, she discovered a small boy walking toward her. She immediately scanned the beach for an adult, but could see no one.

The only house in the direction from which the little boy had come was approximately a half mile away, but it was empty, unless someone had recently bought it.

"Hi," she said, as she reached the child. His face was covered with sand where he'd been crying and wiping the tears with grimy hands. When he looked up at her, she was startled at how beautiful he was. He had eyes the color of blue glass, and the sun reflecting off his hair turned it to the color of glistening gold.

"I want my daddy," he said, between sobs.

"Where's your daddy?" Nella asked, hoping he could remember what direction he needed to go.

"I — don't — know," he sobbed. Nella had to get him calmed down so she could understand what he was saying.

"Which way should we go to find him?" she tried again. The little boy could have come from any direction.

"To my car," he answered. Apparently his father had driven to the beach, but that didn't help, as there were several places accessible for vehicles to drive down to the ocean.

What was she going to do? If she started in one direction looking for the father, he might come from the other direction and miss them. Well, there was only one thing to do: Wait. Sooner or later the child's father would come looking for him — wouldn't he?

Surely this child hadn't been abandoned! NO! She wouldn't even consider that possibility. Letting a child this small get lost on the beach was bad enough. He couldn't be over three years old.

But she couldn't wait long. She was expecting a call from the real estate lady.

Again, she turned and scanned the beach. She thought she caught movement beside a sand dune, but as she looked closer she could see nothing. The beach curved in the opposite direction from which the child had been coming. Maybe that's where the car was parked. Should she try that? No. She decided to stick with her first plan. Wait.

She glanced at her watch. She had thirty minutes before the real estate lady was supposed to call her and set an appointment to show her house tomorrow. She had to think of something fast.

"What's your name?" Nella asked the child, who now seemed content to let her take charge of finding his father

"Jake," he answered. His crying had stopped altogether.

"Jake, where's your father?" she mumbled, mostly to herself, again searching the beach for any sign of human movement, but seeing nothing.

"I told you, I don't know!" The small, impatient voice took Nella by surprise. She looked quickly back at the child, who stood with his hands stretched out in front of him with the palms turned upward as if to emphasize his statement.

Laughter burst from Nella, and the small boy unexpectedly giggled.

He was darling, but Nella couldn't stand here on the beach and wait for the moron who had lost this child. Suddenly, she had an idea.

"Jake, would you like to come up to my house? I'll give you some lemonade, and we can wait for your daddy there. Would you like that?"

"Uh-huh!" he agreed readily.

Nella looked around until she found a piece of driftwood she could write in the sand with, then took the child by the hand and walked back to the steps leading up to her home. She stopped and wrote "Jake" in the sand as large as she could make the letters. Anyone would be able to see the writing from a good distance away. Then she drew an arrow that went from the name to the bottom of the steps that led up to her patio.

She talked to Jake as she worked. "This is your name," she explained. "Your daddy will come looking for you, and he'll see your name and the arrow pointing to my house and he'll come find you."

"Yeah!" The child was confident now that his father would soon find him.

"Who are you, and what are you doing with my son?"

Startled, Nella's eyes flew open from the relaxed nap she had drifted into. She became aware of the sleeping child lying on her stomach and breast, and the tall, angry man towering above her. The sun reflected off his shiny dark hair and picked up the golden flecks in his unusual, light brown eyes, almost giving Nella the sensation some large eagle had swooped down upon her.

Just as she reached to wake the sleeping child, he raised his head slowly and looked at her. His blue eyes were huge and beautiful from the sleep he'd just left. He smiled and patted her face, then saw the man above them.

"Daddy, Daddy," his small voice was excited. "I've found us a new fwend! She gave me some yemonade and it made me feel much better. Then we waited for you to find me."

The stranger reached down and lifted the little boy in his arms, but never took his eyes off Nella as she slowly sat up.

"Well, do you intend to answer my question?" The unusual golden brown eyes held heavy sarcasm, and so did the deep voice.

Nella glanced at her watch and realized that a solid thirty minutes had passed while she dozed. Jake had tired quickly after drinking the cold lemonade, and had soon fallen asleep on her lap. Her eyes had grown weary of searching the beach from her vantage point, so she had lain back in the lounge chair just to rest her eyes, but she, too, had soon dozed off.

Suddenly, she was the one who felt sarcasm creep into her voice.

"Mister, your child can't be over three years old. How long did it take you to realize he was missing? Don't you know what can happen to a child on the beach?" Just thinking of the possibilities horrified Nella, and as she talked she became angrier.

"But he's not on the beach. He's here at a complete stranger's house, and I've been searching frantically for him. What are you doing with him?"

Nella resented the accusing sound of his voice, but tried to hold her temper. "Did you find my message?" she asked calmly.

"Yes, such as it was." His tone was condescending.

"Did it lead you up here?"

"Yes."

"Then it must have been sufficient to help you find your son."

"But it would have been better if you'd waited on the beach with him instead of bringing him up to your home. That's almost like kidnapping." The accusing tone was back.

"That's the most ridiculous thing I have ever heard!" Nella's voice had started to rise. "If I were trying to kidnap him, would I have

5

gone to the trouble of leaving you a message how to find him? I think 'neglect' is the word we're looking for here, not 'kidnapping.'"

"Look," he interrupted. "I didn't mean to be so abrupt, but it was a surprise to find my son at a stranger's house, and asleep on top of her, at that. And, yes, it's been too long without my knowing where he was, but I just got him back from his grandparents today, and I'm not used to having to keep up with an active child. Even so, I don't believe I need a total stranger to tell me how to care for him. Thank you for keeping him until I got here." He picked the small child up and went briskly down the steps.

Nella watched as he disappeared down the beach. She couldn't believe what had just taken place. She thought about the two briefly, then forgot them as she stared at the lapping waves that rolled onto the shore below her.

Two months ago, she had been visiting a friend in Dallas, Texas when she received a phone call that her father had suffered a massive heart attack and was dead. She immediately flew back home to South Carolina, and the following weeks were a nightmare.

She had loved her father dearly and losing him was devastating, but she was also informed that he had accumulated many debts, and the house she had grown up in and loved so much would have to be sold to settle the estate.

Nella had no brothers and sisters, and her mother had died giving birth to her, so all she had was her father and her home.

Now they both would soon be gone.

Nella had been out of college for six months. Her father had suggested she just relax and enjoy life for a little while before trying to get settled into a job. She could just hear him saying, "Once you start working, you'll have to do it the rest of your life." Her father knew she'd have to leave home again and search for work in a larger city. She smiled sadly, knowing he was just trying to keep her close to him as long as possible.

Nella knew she could move into Charleston and get a job there. She always enjoyed going to Charleston to shop. That's where the people in her small community went when they wanted to get a touch of "city life." She loved Charleston, with its old homes, streets, and parks that still had the flavor of the days when the city was the social, political, and economic hub of the royal province of Carolina, with the many features that attracted tourists each year. She especially loved the azaleas in the spring. But she just didn't want to live and work there. At this point, though, it didn't seem as if she had a choice.

She went inside and wandered around the house for a long time, touching the beloved walls that had sheltered her from so many storms, looking out the windows at the scenic views, and remembering her childhood and all the happy days she'd spent playing on the beach. Finally she went to bed to cry herself to sleep. The real estate lady would be here at ten o'clock in the morning with a prospective buyer for her home.

At nine fifty-nine, the doorbell rang. Nella went to answer the door with a mixture of dismay and curiosity. Although she dreaded the ordeal before her, she was anxious to see who'd want to purchase her beloved home.

Nothing could have prepared her for the man and child who stood before her with the real estate lady.

"Look, Daddy, our new fwend." The blue eyes sparkled up at Nella as the child promptly stepped through the doorway and took her hand.

"Jake! You're supposed to wait until you're invited in." The stern voice caused the little boy to quickly jump back beside his father and stare wide-eyed at Nella.

In spite of her sadness, Nella couldn't restrain a little smile as she said, "Please, do come in."

"Miss Covington," the tall, thin real estate lady spoke first. "This is Samuel L. du Cannon, and his son Jake. They've just recently decided to relocate to our community, and Mr. du Cannon would like to look at your house. Mr. du Cannon, this is Nella Covington."

The man looked different standing in her home. He was tall. Probably an inch or two over six feet. His hair was very dark, maybe even black, with a peppering of gray in the temples. Again, she was keenly aware of the golden brown eyes. One shade lighter and they'd be yellow! Uncanny, she thought. A dark, neatly trimmed mustache covered his top lip. His lips were well shaped, as if a sculptor had chiseled them to perfection. Not too thin, yet not too thick. He was, she mused resentfully to herself, a very handsome man.

She made no attempt to shake hands with him or to even acknowledge the introduction. She knew she was being rude, but, after all, she owed him one from yesterday.

"Did you know you were coming here today when we talked yesterday?" Now her voice was accusing.

"No. I knew Miss James was going to show me a house today, but I had no idea where it was." He hoped his answer sounded genuine.

The real estate lady was surprised they'd already met, and was about to ask a question when Nella shrugged and said, "Show Mr. du

Cannon around. I'll be on the patio when you're finished." And she turned and left them. There was no way she could follow two strangers around as they analyzed the good and bad points of her beloved home.

She sank slowly into a patio chair and closed her eyes.

"Oh, Daddy, how could you have allowed this to happen to me?" She would have felt bitterness toward her father had she not loved him so much.

She wished she knew what problems he'd encountered to allow things to get this far out of hand. He hadn't had any health problems that she was aware of. In fact, the heart attack had been sudden, with no warning signals. Even the family accountant hadn't been able to give her any answers as to why the finances had been in such bad shape. It wasn't her college expenditures, as she had gone to college on a full scholarship, and had earned spending money by typing papers for other students while she was in college.

She should have spent more time discussing business matters with her father. That brought a smile to her lips, for she knew full well he would never have "burdened" her with financial problems. He was of the old school that men should take care of the household and the "women folk."

Nella felt a tear run down her cheek as she remembered the tenderness he always showed her. Now she had no one. She would have had Nick, but they'd broken off their engagement months ago. Their goals had become farther and farther apart until they both realized they didn't have a future together.

"Now, today, you cry." The small voice showed great concern.

Nella opened her tear-filled eyes to see the angelic face close to hers. The blond hair, which curled softly, glistened in the morning sunlight. Again, Nella was in awe of the rich golden color.

"Yesterday, I cry. Today, you cry. Want me to sit on your yap and make you feel better?"

Nella smiled, and the smile she received in return was mixed with a giggle. She felt her heart fill with warmth.

"Yes, Jake, I would love for you to sit on my lap and make me feel better."

After settling in to his satisfaction, the small face turned up to Nella.

"Why are you sad?" he asked, as he held her thumb in his hand and plucked at her thumbnail with his finger, his eyes never leaving hers.

"I'm sad because I miss my father and because I have to sell my home." Nella answered the child honestly.

"I miss my mama. Daddy says she went to Heaven, and she can't come back, but she's with me whenever I think about her, my daddy says. Hey, I know what!" As quickly as the sadness had come, it was replaced with his new idea. "If my daddy buys your house, you can come and live with us! You and me can be fwends for never and never!"

Nella was surprised at how well this small boy could talk and put his thoughts into words. Someone had spent a lot of time with him. He was very intelligent.

She was about to explain why she couldn't do what he suggested when she looked up into a pair of golden brown eyes.

"Is that his idea, or yours?" There was no mistaking the accusation in the voice.

Nella was instantly angry. Slowly and very gently she stood the child down from her lap and rose from the chair. Stretching to her tallest five-foot-seven-inch height, she stared daggers into the arrogant man's eyes. "Sir, you are quite despicable!"

At that moment the real estate lady came through the door, not noticing the tension in the air.

"Okay, Miss Covington. Mr. du Cannon has decided to take the house, so we're going over to my office to draw up the contract. He'll present his offer and the three of us can go over it. Will two o'clock Friday be okay with you?"

"Yes, yes, that's fine," Nella agreed quickly. She just wanted these people to be gone.

As the car drove away, Jake waved from the back window until the car was out of sight. How could such a loathsome man father such an adorable child, Nella wondered?

She turned back inside and looked around miserably. She knew she should start packing, but she just couldn't bring herself to do it yet. Instead, she went to the phone and called her best friend, Julie.

"Julie, can I come over and bring a cheap bottle of wine? I need to unwind and talk."

"Nella? It's only eleven forty-five in the morning."

"I know, but I do need to talk. I'm signing the closing contract on the house Friday."

Now the voice on the line was full of concern. "Oh, baby, I'm so sorry! You come on over, and don't bother about bringing wine. I've got some real expensive stuff here. We'll have lunch and drink wine until you feel a lot better!"

Friday came much too soon. Nella reluctantly parked her car and walked slowly toward the real estate office.

As she entered the plush office a small, familiar figure ran toward her. "Hi Nel — uh, Miss Cubington! Daddy said I shouldn't call you Nella. I must call you Miss Cubington."

"Jake! Please come sit down!" Sam du Cannon tried not to sound too impatient with the child.

As Nella settled into a chair, she smiled at the boy. He was such a darling child. Too bad he'd probably grow up to be unbearable like his father.

As she watched him he quietly slipped away from his father, who was in deep discussion with the real estate lady, and came to her. In a conspiratorial whisper, he asked, "Can I sit on your yap?"

Just as quietly, Nella lifted him and settled him on her lap. He snuggled back against her and became instantly quiet and content.

When the other two people finished their conversation, Sam du Cannon looked up and spotted Jake on Nella's lap. She saw a flash of emotion in those strange-colored eyes. It wasn't anger, but she didn't try to analyze it. She imagined those eyes could wreak havoc on a woman if he decided to turn on the charm. She could almost imagine how warmly they'd glow if he were speaking soft words of love. She mentally shook herself off that disturbing train of thought.

He seemed about to speak to the boy, then changed his mind as the real estate lady started discussing the closing of the contract on the property that was once her haven, her escape, her home.

Nella barely listened to the drone of voices as they went on and on. She knew the seemingly efficient Mr. Du Cannon would see to it that everything was in proper order.

"Miss Covington? Miss Covington?" She was brought out of her deep concentration by the real estate lady's persistent voice. "You need to sign where I've made the Xs."

As Nella leaned forward to sign the stack of papers in front of her, she realized that her lap burden had sat very quietly through the long, boring transaction. But now, his father stood and lifted him from her lap. His hand brushed hers as he lifted the child. She was aware of, and irritated with, the bolt of electricity his touch sent coursing up her hand and arm.

They all shook hands and said the appropriate things. Nella headed for her car. Her hand was on the car door handle when a voice from behind stopped her.

"Miss Covington?"

She turned to face the man, wondering what he could possibly want now. She didn't have time to hide the tears rolling down her cheeks.

This time there was surprise in his eyes, then something a lot like compassion, which was the last thing she wanted to see. She wanted to shout "what do you want?" but the lump in her throat kept her from uttering a sound.

"Miss Covington, there's a small restaurant around the corner. Will you come and have lunch with Jake and me? There's — " here he paused, as if uncertain whether to go on or not, then continued, "there's something I want to discuss with you." As he talked, he'd taken a handkerchief from his pocket and wiped the tears from her face. She tried to turn her face away, but he firmly held her chin and gently wiped all the tear stains away.

She was about to decline the lunch invitation when a small hand tucked inside hers and a pleading little voice said, "Please come, Miss Cubington — please."

Nella smiled at the upturned face, then looked at the man in front of her. "I don't know what you could possibly want to discuss with me, but okay, I'll have lunch with you."

Settled in a booth in the restaurant, Nella smiled behind her menu as the little boy beside her studied his menu and pretended to be reading it.

"I want a hambooger and fryers," he stated in a matter-of-fact voice.

"Don't you think you need some vegetables?" his father asked.

"I don't want any vegbables, Daddy." His pleading eyes and face would have been hard for the toughest heart to resist.

"Okay." His father smiled and agreed reluctantly, "but next time we'd better have vegetables."

It was the first time Nella had seen the man smile, and she was dumbfounded at the change it made in him. His facial features softened, and if Nella had thought him handsome earlier, he was surely breathtaking now. To keep from staring at him she went swiftly back to studying her menu.

After the waitress had taken the orders, Sam looked directly at Nella for the first time since they'd sat down. "Miss Covington, I have a proposition I want to discuss with you. Now, please hear me out before you object. When I'm finished we can discuss any questions or objections that you might have.

"Jake's mother died one year ago. She and I had grown apart prior to that, but for Jake's sake we'd remained together longer than we should have. Her parents have never approved of me and they were constantly encouraging her to break up the marriage. They never thought I was good enough for Vanessa. Last year, when I was out of town on one of my business trips, Vanessa was involved in a car accident and she was dead on arrival at the hospital. Naturally her parents believed that if I'd been home like a good husband, she would never have been out in *that* car, at *that* time of night, with *that* man. In their minds, the wreck and the fact that they lost their daughter was entirely my fault. They could never believe any wrong of their little girl.

"They're determined to take custody of Jake. They don't believe I'll be a good father because I travel a lot with my business, and they don't want their grandson to be raised by nannies and strangers.

"I can see their point of view to a certain degree, but a lot of children have been raised by a loving nanny.

"At any rate, they have the best lawyer they can find on the case. He's good, too. I know him by reputation, and he'll turn over every stone for some small piece of dirt to hang on me. So far he's found nothing, but if I should ever slip up, or if he can make it look like I've slipped up, then I'll lose my son forever, and I just can't take that chance.

"I've had an idea in the back of my head now for some time, and I think you've furnished the missing piece. You see, I don't ever intend on becoming involved with another woman on a long-term basis. Sure, I'm a normal man, but with a good bit of precaution, a man can lead a normal life and find someone occasionally to relieve his tensions."

Nella could not believe how cold and hard this man must be. He spoke as if he had no heart at all. The only time she saw a hint of softness and compassion was when he talked to his son.

15

"Anyway," he continued, "Jake does need a woman's touch. He needs a mother, if you will, and surely not that bitch of a grandmother. I quiver to think of him being raised and influenced by her."

Nella was dumbfounded that he was talking like this in front of Jake. Maybe his in-laws had a point. But she listened as he continued.

"So, for some time, now, I've been thinking about what kind of woman I need to fill the bill of a mother for Jake — and Miss Covington, I think you're the one. Especially since Jake seems so taken with you."

Nella started to speak, but he raised his hands to stop her.

"No, hear me out. You see, if you marry me, you'll be able to stay in your beloved home. Of course, we won't share the same bedroom, as this is strictly a business deal. So we'll all be winners here. You'll get to keep your home, Jake gets a mother, and I won't have to ever worry about being attracted to you."

Nella stared at the man in silence until he raised his eyebrows in a questioning gesture.

"Oh, may I speak now?"

He only nodded.

"What do you mean about never being attracted to me?"

His chuckle was genuine.

"Well, I never have been, nor will I ever be, attracted to a large woman. Oh, I like women with a good, healthy looking body, but not too much body."

Nella could only stare at the man in stunned silence. She had been a chubby child who had grown into a plus-sized woman. But she had been raised to be proud of herself, to be as healthy as possible, to look her best, and, most of all, to be proud of her heritage — part of which was a plus-sized mother and grandmother. All the family pictures her father had kept through the years had shown a family history of plus-sized women, and she never questioned the fact that she had inherited the genes they all carried and handed down to her.

Nella had been told on numerous occasions that she was a beautiful woman. She had turned many heads with her long auburn hair, her smoky blue eyes, and her hourglass body. Although she was large, she'd always been proud of her body, and had always taken care of herself. She wasn't about to let this man's misguided opinion upset her. Even though he was trying to be discreet in his wording, she could sense what he was actually saying.

She was about to tell him in no uncertain terms what she felt for him when two small arms circled her neck. She glanced around at the beautiful little boy standing on the seat beside her. His face was close to hers, and suddenly he kissed her on the lips.

"Well, are you gonna marry us? I'll be so happy if you do. I don't want to live with my 'nother grandmother. She makes me go to bed-out with my goodnight milk when I'm bad. And sometimes I can't help but be bad when I'm with her."

Nella knew she was a fool, but what did she have to lose? Her father was dead. Her engagement was off. And she didn't have a home or a job. She had nowhere to go, and no one to turn to. If she went with this plan, she could stay in her home, at least until she decided she couldn't stand to be in the presence of this man any-more, and she would surely be appreciated and loved by Jake. Hopefully Sam would stay gone most of the time on business trips and she wouldn't have to see him except on his occasional trip home. Then his time would be taken up with Jake, so she still wouldn't have to see him that much. Undoubtedly she could stand him on that basis. Especially when she thought of all the other benefits.

She thought her heart would pound out of her chest as she made her decision. She looked up at the man who sat patiently waiting as if he knew what her answer would be. Then she looked at the little boy who still had his arms around her neck.

"I'll consider it, but I have to have at least until this time tomorrow to give you an answer." Her voice shook as she spoke.

"What does that mean, Daddy? Is she or not?"

"She will."

Nella wanted to reach across the table and slap his arrogant, handsome face, but she kept still, knowing he was probably correct. But she wasn't going to give him the satisfaction of agreeing on the spot.

The child gave a shriek of joy and said at the top of his voice, "Hey eberybody, Miss Cubington's gonna marry us!"

And as if on cue, the people in the surrounding area applauded and cheered. That made Jake even happier. As they left the restaurant, he was jumping about and giggling with joy.

As they reached the cars parked side by side, Sam du Cannon spoke. "We'll just go back to our respective dwellings for the night. I'll contact you tomorrow and you can tell me what your decision is. I think it'll be a major advantage to all of us if you do agree to this."

He was already in charge of her life. Nella could not believe she was actually contemplating this stupid undertaking.

"Oh, and Miss Covington, I noticed that you ordered the lite plate at lunch. Please don't feel like you have to eat cottage cheese and fruit when you're with me. Just continue to be yourself."

Angrier than she had been in a long time, Nella's voice trembled with emotion when she answered him.

"Mr. du Cannon, I have never, nor shall I ever change my lifestyle to try to impress you or anyone else, no matter how pumped up you are with your own importance! You are, without a doubt, the most pompous, arrogant bigot I have ever run across in all of my twenty-five years. Why I'm agreeing to even consider spending one more second with you is beyond me. I truly must be out of my mind."

And with that, she slid into her little red Volkswagen and ground the gears out of the parking lot.

Sam du Cannon stood for a few moments beside his black late-model Rolls Royce and pondered her temper tantrum.

He had first seen Nella in the grocery store a couple of weeks ago. She'd been talking to a young woman with a small child, and Sam had been drawn to her by the expression on her face as she talked to the baby. Her eyes had held a soft glow as she talked, and the baby was obviously responding to her as it cooed and smiled back at her. Sam felt at once that she would make a good mother, so he waited until she went through the checkout line, then asked the lady checking groceries if she knew Nella. The woman assured Sam that Nella was single.

But before asking Nella to marry him, he'd talked with several of the leading people in the community concerning her quality of character and her morals. Everyone had praised her. Everyone knew her and her father, and spoke very highly of them. He'd even set her up yesterday, when he deliberately let her think he'd lost track of Jake. He'd been watching them all along from behind a sand dune. He wanted to see how she'd handle a sticky situation, and she had handled it quite impressively. Who would have thought about leaving a message in the sand like that? And Jake had obviously taken to her instantly.

That's why he'd thought he'd found the perfect solution for his son's life. A small community to grow up in and a good, solid woman to raise and influence him.

He really hadn't meant any harm by the statements he'd made about her size. In fact, for Jake's sake, that was a good thing. He'd always heard people like her were easy-going and jolly.

But this temper thing — he shook his head in concern as he got into his car. He'd have to speak with her about that.

When Nella stopped her car she realized she was in front of Julie's apartment. She almost never stopped by Julie's without calling first. She was careful to never take advantage of her friendship, but she was too angry at this point to consider anything except talking with someone who really cared how she felt.

"He *whaaat?*" Julie couldn't believe what Nella was telling her.

"You heard me. He wants me to marry him so he can have a mother for his son. His in-laws are trying to prove he's an unfit parent, and he thinks if he has a wife it'll be harder for them to find something against him. Oh, and get this. He made it very clear that he won't have a problem being attracted to me because he doesn't like large women."

"No! He didn't say that! What a jerk! Well, obviously you said no, didn't you?"

"I told him I'd think about it."

"Nella! Are you crazy? You'd have to be out of your mind to agree to his proposal. You can just get that out of your head right now. As your best friend, I won't sit by and let you make that kind of mistake." Julie was adamant with disgust.

"But Julie, listen to me. I could keep my house. I wouldn't have to worry about moving into Charleston and finding work that I'd probably hate. I'd just be a glorified nanny to Jake. And Julie, that is the most precious child I've ever seen. I think I already love him."

"It sounds like you already have your mind made up." Julie's voice was filled with disbelief.

"No, I haven't decided yet, but there are some good points to think about. If I don't have to be around this Sam person much, it won't be a bad arrangement at all. He travels with his work, so he'll be gone most of the time. It would just be Jake and me at home, and that would be wonderful."

"Nella, if you're really considering this, at least call Sheriff Dansby and see if he'll run a profile check on this man. For all you know he could be some kind of criminal." Julie's voice was so full of concern that Nella agreed to let her call the sheriff.

Luckily the department was having a slow day, so the deputy took the information and did the check while Julie waited on the phone. It only took a few minutes before the deputy came back on the line. Nella watched Julie's face change expression.

"No!" she said in disbelief. "Really? *WOW!*"

Now Nella was concerned. Maybe Sam du Cannon was a ruthless killer. What a mistake it'd be to get involved with someone like that! She was glad Julie had made the call. Just before Nella was convinced the stranger needed to go straight to jail, Julie hung up the phone.

"You are not going to believe who this man is!"

"What? What? Is he a criminal? Is he an escaped convict? What?" Nella's impatience made her jumble her words.

21

"He's probably the wealthiest man in Charleston. He's the owner of one of the largest seafood chains in the nation. If you marry that man, you'll be one wealthy woman. And I've changed my mind totally. I say go for it! You deserve all the happiness you can find."

"But Julie," Nella reminded her, "this won't be 'happiness' if I decide to do this. It'll only be 'security.'"

"So how much different are the two? You know, really?" Julie had always been more materialistic than Nella.

"For me there's a lot of difference," Nella assured her. "I'd rather be happy with someone I love and not have anything, than own millions of dollars and not be with someone I really love."

"So what are you going to do in the meantime, while you wait for this special person to love? Where are you going to live? What are you going to do for a living?" On any other occasion, Julie's total change of attitude would have been humorous.

"I don't know yet. I don't know what I should do." Nella felt her head would explode from unmade decisions. She said good-by and left her friend's house.

As she pulled her car into the driveway of her beloved home, the sun was setting. The scattered clouds reflected beautiful purple and blue hues, with streaks of red mingled in here and there. All blended with the ocean, turning the view into her own gorgeous oil painting.

She knew instantly what her decision would be. She would keep her home, at whatever cost, for as long as she could.

Chapter 2

They'd been married for four weeks. Sam had left on a business trip two days after they were married. Jake had been totally content to stay with Nella, and didn't seem to miss his father much at all.

Nella had never known how active a three-year-old could be. Her days were spent answering endless questions about everything in general. She read to him, she played everything from cowboys to building blocks, and, to her amazement, found she loved every minute of it.

She smiled down at the small, sleeping bundle as he lay curled in his bed. In this short time she'd lost her heart forever to this little human being. All he had to do was smile at her and she was putty in his hands. He was beginning to realize that, too, and was using it to his advantage.

When Jake woke up Nella made him breakfast and helped him dress. She had to go into town and run some errands, and she wanted to go early, while he was still fresh and rested from his night's sleep.

She'd visited several stores before Jake started getting tired and cranky. She was basically finished with all the shopping she needed to do, so she decided to leave the rest undone and go home. She'd tried once before to shop with Jake when he wasn't in a very good mood, and it only proved to be disastrous, so she didn't want to push her luck today.

They were almost to her Volkswagen when Jake asked, "Can we get a yogurt, Nella?" They were passing a coffee shop that served frozen yogurt, and Jake remembered going inside the last time they were in town.

She took time to put the packages in her car first. As she closed the trunk, she glanced across the street. A man was casually leaning against a beat-up Ford pickup truck. Had he been staring at her? And did he look quickly away? Nella was accustomed to having men stare at her, but this seemed different. This man was sleazy — no other word suited him better. Just sleazy.

"Come on, Nella." Jake was tugging at her hand.

She followed him into the shop, where they each enjoyed a cone of frozen yogurt. Nella forgot about the man across the street as Jake chatted about things they'd seen that morning. He had a hard time trying to keep the yogurt from running down and getting on his hand, and couldn't enjoy the cone because he hated having sticky hands. Nella made a mental note to get their yogurt in cups next time. By the time they'd finished Jake was almost dozing in his chair, so she picked him up and carried him to the car.

Just as she reached for the car door handle she looked up into the bleary eyes of the sleazeball from across the street But now he was very close, and he was reaching for Jake. "Gimmie the boy, lady. I'm taking him home."

As he touched Jake the boy cried out and grabbed Nella tightly around the neck. Nella clutched him closely to her chest and raised her knee into Sleazeball's crotch with as much force as she could muster. He yelped in surprise and doubled over in pain.

Nella quickly shoved Jake into the Volkswagen and left the scene with screeching tires. As she turned the corner she glanced in the rearview mirror and saw the man was still bent over, holding himself.

Arriving home, Nella rushed inside the house and locked the door behind her. Jake knew she was upset, so he was crying a little, but she sat him down on the couch and ran to do a double check on all the other doors and windows to see if they were locked. She knew she couldn't become a prisoner in her own home, but she had to feel safe until she could figure out what to do next.

She sat down and held Jake closely in her lap. He lay against her and started to settle down.

Who was that jerk? Would he come back? Why did he want Jake? She was so frightened now by what could have happened back there that she was trembling all over.

Jake soon fell asleep, so she laid him gently on the couch beside her. She couldn't even imagine what kind of wrath Sam du Cannon would have heaped upon her if she'd allowed that stranger to kidnap his son. Just the thought of those eyes burning into hers sent shudders down her spine.

She got up and went to the kitchen to get some water. As she passed the phone, she noticed she had messages on her answering machine. The first caller had hung up at the sound of the tone, but the second caller was a deep, familiar voice. "Hi, it's Sam. I'll be home in approximately two hours. It's ten o'clock now."

He must have called right after she left for town. He should be home at any moment, since it was a little past noon.

Nella started to relax. Sam would know how to handle the situation. He might even know who the man was who'd tried to snatch Jake.

Soon she heard a car in the driveway. She looked out the window. Sure enough, it was Sam's Rolls Royce. She opened the door to wait for him.

Suddenly Sheriff Dansby's patrol car screeched to a stop behind Sam's car, and the sheriff jumped out of the car and ran up to Sam.

"Are they okay? Did she get the boy home okay?" Excitement made the sheriff jumble his words.

"What the hell are you talking about, man?" Sam didn't know whether to be concerned or irritated.

Nella came from the house and approached the two men.

"Oh, there you are!" Relief flooded the sheriff's voice. He took a couple of deep breaths to gain control.

Sheriff Dansby was an average-built man with a receding hairline. His eyes were soft blue and kindly. Nella had known him all of her life. He'd been a close friend of her father's.

"Nella, you were fantastic back there." He'd managed to catch his breath. "I saw the whole thing from the hardware store. When you kneed that jerk in the crotch, I couldn't believe it. But I ran and cuffed him while he was still on his knees. Would you like a job as a deputy?"

"Would someone mind telling me what is going on?" Impatience, and a growing anger at being in the dark about a seemingly intense situation, brought a heightened color to Sam's face.

"You don't know, then?" Sheriff Dansby asked the obvious question, and then continued to explain.

"Well, that weasel was waiting on Nella when she started to get in her car. He tried to grab your little boy, but she hung onto your son for dear life and landed her knee right in the ole boy's balls and bent him double. Then she jumped in that car of hers and tore out of town like a bat outa hell. I grabbed the skunk while he was down and cuffed him. After some coaxing, he told me your in-laws had paid him to kidnap the boy and bring him to them. He's still in jail if you want to file charges against him, and them."

"No!" The explosive sound came from Sam. Nella was amazed at the calm fury on his face.

"You let the man go. But you write an extensive report on what happened and keep it on file. My in-laws will hang themselves if given enough rope. They're just that stupid. Thank you for your help, Sheriff," he said, and turned and went into the house.

Sheriff Dansby shrugged his shoulders and asked Nella, "Are you okay?"

"Yes, Harmon, and thanks for checking on me." She reached out and touched his arm as she spoke.

"Nella — " he hesitated, obviously wanting to ask her something, but not sure if he should or not.

"Go ahead, Harmon. What do you want to know?"

"Well, it's none of my business, but why did you marry this stranger? Did you meet him somewhere else? Did — ?" Nella stopped him.

"Harmon, I'm okay. Don't worry about me. You know my father taught me to be a survivor. I will survive, Harmon. I will survive." He didn't like the sad note in her voice that she almost managed to conceal.

Nella kissed his concerned cheek. Then she, too, turned and went inside.

Sam was sitting on the couch beside Jake when she entered the room. He had one of the child's small hands in his. Raw concern made his face pale.

"I'm leaving for Hawaii in three days, and I want you and Jake to go with me."

"But — " she was about to protest when he stopped her.

"No arguments, Nella." His voice was determined and final. My in-laws will not stop at anything until they get what they want, and they want Jake. So until this blows over, I want you and Jake with me on every trip I make."

"Sam, I don't think — " Again she tried to protest, but again she was cut short.

"Just pack, Nella. Just pack." Suddenly his voice sounded tired.

Later in her room, she admitted to herself she and Jake would be safer being with Sam for a while, but she couldn't even imagine how hard it was going to be to travel with him all the time.

She stopped in the middle of what she was doing. Would they share one hotel room? One bed? How on earth would Sam work all of this out?

This was not at all what she'd envisioned when she agreed to the marriage. She never dreamed she'd have to leave her home and travel with Sam. Now what? Should she just call the whole thing off before it went any further?

But what about Jake?

Suddenly she knew she'd already gone too far. In these short weeks, Jake's best interests had become much more important to her than her own. Groaning inwardly, she finished the packing.

The flight to Honolulu was uneventful, and now in the luxurious hotel suite Nella smiled as she unpacked Jake's and her clothes. Sam had taken Jake to walk on the beach so Nella could have some time to get things in order. At least that's the excuse he'd given to get Jake to himself for a while.

They were in a big, beautiful suite that contained a living space, a kitchenette, and three bedrooms. The furniture was solid mahogany, and there was enough space for three more people.

And she'd worried that they'd be in a single motel room! She should have known Sam du Cannon would only settle for the best.

Nella made up her mind to enjoy every moment of this. This was the type of luxury most people only dreamed of, and never got to actually experience. Well, her chance was here and she meant to enjoy it! She planned to see as much of Honolulu as possible, and maybe even some of the surrounding islands.

In a little while she heard Sam and Jake returning. As soon as Sam opened the door, Jake ran to her.

"Nella, look what I founded." He was clutching several small shells in his hands. "I brought them to you. Do you like them?"

"Oh, I love them. They're beautiful." Nella knelt in front of the child and made a big deal over the gift he'd brought her. He beamed with pleasure that his gift was so well received.

Nella looked up and caught Sam watching the exchange between her and Jake with a concerned expression on his face.

Later, as Jake napped, Sam sat in a recliner reading the paper and Nella settled down at the dining room table to paint her nails. She was intent on what she was doing and didn't know how long Sam had been standing by her, watching her, when she looked up into his face. He wore the same concerned look that she had seen earlier.

"I hope I haven't made a big mistake in bringing you and Jake together." He pulled out a chair and sat down.

"Why do you say that?" Nella blew on her nails to dry them faster.

"Nella, when he's with you, you're the only thing he's interested in, and when he's not with you, he talks about you constantly. He seems to adore you, and I've watched you with him. In this short time you seem to love him more than his mother ever appeared to."

"Well, I don't profess to be a psychologist, but I think it's perfectly normal for a child his age to need a mother figure around, and after having lost his mom, he'd just naturally hold on to someone a little harder than normal. There may be a subconscious fear that I'll leave him, too."

"That's what I'm concerned about. If the time should come that you need to go, will I have done more damage to my son than if I'd just tried to fight the odds and raise him by myself?"

"In my opinion, it's better to have known someone and loved them as much as possible and then lose them than to never know what it's like to have known that love. Just like the old saying, 'it's better to have loved and lost than never to have loved at all.' Remember, I grew up without a mother, and I used to go to sleep each night fantasizing about what my mom and I would have done that day, if she could have been with me."

The sadness in her voice and the tears in her eyes reminded Sam that her childhood had been incomplete because she didn't have a mother around. Maybe he'd made the right decision. He surely hoped so.

Just then Jake came from the bedroom, rubbing the sleep from his eyes. He smiled and went straight to Nella. She lifted him to her lap and held him closely as he wrapped his arms around her neck and laid his head on her shoulder.

Her eyes met Sam's over the child's head, and he smiled at her. It was the first time he'd ever looked her directly in the eyes and smiled. Her heart tried to leap up through her throat. She had a tiny premonition of trouble ahead.

Each passing day she became more and more aware of how handsome Sam du Cannon was. She reminded herself often that she needed to be thinking about anything else besides how good he looked after he'd just had a shower and his hair still lay damp and dark against his tanned forehead. Or how the muscles rippled in his arms when he lifted Jake to his lap. Or how sexy he looked when he came in at night and took off his tie and undid the first few buttons on his shirt to let a sprinkling of dark chest hair spiral from the opening.

Chapter 3

Life settled into a comfortable enough routine during the following few weeks. Nella got up at six o'clock every morning and went to the beach to swim while Sam had coffee, read the paper, and got dressed for work. By the time he was ready to leave for work Nella was back from her swim, ready to start her day in her role as super-nanny. At night, she usually fixed their evening meal in the hotel suite. Occasionally Sam worked late and she only had to worry about making food for Jake and herself. A few nights they had eaten in one of the family restaurants in the hotel.

This morning when the alarm went off, Nella woke up to an old, familiar heaviness in her lower abdomen. Cramps. She also felt blah and listless. She reset the alarm for seven o'clock. No swimming this morning. She'd just go back to sleep, and when she got up, Sam would be gone.

She smiled with the satisfaction of a well-made decision and was soon sound asleep. It seemed only moments later that the alarm went off again, and she reluctantly got up.

She needed to have a cup of coffee to get awake before Jake woke up to start his day. Yawning and rubbing her eyes, she stumbled into the kitchen/dining area.

She was in the middle of the room before she discovered Sam sitting at the table, his coffee cup half raised to his lips and the paper in front of him.

"Oh!" she exclaimed, becoming acutely aware that her hair was a mess from the previous night's sleep, and that she hadn't bothered to put on her robe. The nightgown she wore was black with a lacy, fitted bodice that covered approximately one third of her large breasts, then flowed in layers to the floor. But what did she care? He'd made it plain he wouldn't be affected by her one way or the other.

"What are you doing here? I thought you'd be at work by now."

"I'm going in later today. I thought you'd be swimming."

There was coffee still in the pot, so she poured a cup and sat down at the table and reached for part of the paper. Normally she would have gone and put her robe on, but today she refused to retreat. Sam had said he wouldn't be attracted to her, so it wouldn't matter if she sat here in the nude.

"You're just going to sit there dressed like that?" Their eyes met across the table.

"Why not?" she asked, not wavering.

"You're half naked." His sweeping glance took in the part of her body above the table.

"And you're not?" Her eyes roved casually over his shirtless torso. All he had on was slacks. His chest was covered in a dark mass of curly hair. She felt a tiny chill go up her spine, and knew her nipples were getting hard, but her gaze never left his.

"That's different, I'm a man!" His retort was serious, and he was becoming angry.

"Oh. You're a man, and that makes it okay. Well, it doesn't matter, anyway. You said fat women didn't turn you on." She knew she was agitating him, and she realized she was enjoying it.

"Actually, what I said," now he was tightlipped, "was that I'm not attracted to large women. I would prefer that you don't put words in my mouth."

Her only answer was a shrug as she lifted the coffee cup to her lips. She saw his gaze fall to her cleavage and linger there momentarily.

Suddenly he slammed his cup to the table and with an angry grunt left the room. She heard his bedroom door slam. Smiling, she picked up the paper.

Sam stood in the middle of his bedroom. What had just happened? Had he just had an argument and lost? He didn't like this feeling at all. He was a powerful man. The people in his world didn't have the audacity to argue with him, much less argue and win.

She was right, though. He'd told her he wouldn't ever have to worry about being attracted to her. Then why was he standing in the middle of his bedroom, fully aroused?

Nella heard the shower being turned on in his bathroom, and hoped the water was cold. She heard Jake stirring, waking up in the other room. She put on her robe and went to his bedroom.

He lay in the middle of the full-sized bed, looking lost among all the covers. His big blue eyes watched her walk in. She loved the way he looked in the morning. She loved watching him come awake and get ready for his busy day.

Jake liked her to lie beside him and read him a story when he woke up. That's what they did each morning. He seemed to do better during the day if they started the day with some quiet time together. As she lay on the bed beside him and read to him, Jake twirled a strand of her hair around and around his small hand.

She didn't know how long Sam had been standing there when she closed the book and looked up, but she was taken aback by the gentle expression in his eyes.

"Daddy!" Jake yelped and leaped for his father.

Sam laughed and dropped his briefcase in time to catch the flying bundle that came toward him.

He looked breathtaking in his dark gray three-piece suit. But suddenly Nella had a flashback of how he'd looked earlier without a shirt on. That was one memory she needed to lose.

That afternoon Sam called and told Nella not to make dinner, that they would eat out.

They had a nice meal in a small restaurant, with Jake doing most of the talking. When they started to leave the cashier handed Jake a lollipop and asked if he wanted it. He looked up at Nella hesitantly. "Will just one make my teeth rot out?"

Sam exploded with laughter, but Nella managed to maintain a straight face. "I guess one will be okay," she told him.

Back in the room, Jake got busy playing with a new toy Sam had brought him. Nella was getting his bed ready to tuck him in for the night when Sam came into the room.

"The office staff is throwing a party Friday night. They want to celebrate the opening of our new facility here. They've been after me to let them meet you, so I'd like for you to plan to come with me."

"Won't that be awkward for you?" Nella wondered how he felt about having to introduce his plus-sized wife to everyone.

"I'll take care of myself. Just be ready to go at seven o'clock. Oh, and it's kind of dress up, but not really formal — do you need to shop?"

"Well, actually, I *will* need to shop. I didn't come prepared to party." She had plenty of clothes for all occasions at home, but she hadn't planned to be going out much, under the circumstances.

"I called the babysitting service here at the hotel today. Jake can stay with them." As usual, he had everything under control.

He was leaving the room when he turned back to her.

"Oh, and thank you for teaching Jake that candy will rot his teeth," he said, a slight smile playing around the corners of his mouth.

Then he added more seriously, "I'll admit, when I made our arrangement with you, Jake's diet was the only thing I was concerned about. But you aren't at all like I expected."

"You mean because I don't lie around all day on the couch and eat junk food? And because I exercise, and try to be healthy?"

She knew she was being blunt, but with this subject she meant to be blunt. He was like so many others who had a false concept of fat people.

"Yes, I guess that's what I mean." To her amazement, he looked embarrassed.

"Sam, I don't mean to be unkind about this, but you're just one of a multitude of people who have been brainwashed into believing the wrong thing about fat people. You see, I inherited my size, just like I inherited the color of my eyes, the shape of my nose, my height — well, you get the picture."

She would have gone on, but just then Jake bounded into the room wanting to know if he could sleep with his new toy.

The next night, Sam asked Jake if he'd like to go to the beach the next day and have a picnic. Jake was instantly excited, and started bounding around making plans that included Nella. Finally she stopped him.

"Jake, maybe your daddy wants just you and him to go on a picnic. I think he wants to spend some time with you." She assumed Sam wanted a day out with his son.

"Why don't you want to go?" Sam asked from across the room, where he sat in a recliner, watching the evening news. He muted the TV to wait for her answer.

"Well — I just assumed — " she stammered, taken by surprise at his questioning look.

"Well, you assumed incorrectly," he informed her. "I want this to be a family outing for Jake's sake. He needs to get the feeling he belongs to a family."

"Yeah, Nella, we're fambly, so you're coming, okay?" His decision seemed to be made.

"Okay," Nella agreed. She glanced at Sam, but he was already listening to something on the TV.

The next day was beautiful. The sky was a magnificent azure blue, with a spattering of white clouds pushed along by a playful breeze. The temperature was perfect for a picnic. Not too hot, yet warm enough for a comfortable swim.

Sam led them to a spot that was secluded from the rest of the people on the beach. It was like their very own private little haven. Jake conned his father into building a sand castle, so Nella slipped out of the wrap she'd worn over her bathing suit and headed for the water.

"Be careful," Sam called over his shoulder, and continued to help Jake.

The water engulfed Nella as she dove into an oncoming wave. She loved swimming so much, she was convinced sometimes she'd originally descended from a mermaid. She swam until she became tired, then headed back to shore.

When she returned she saw Sam sitting in the water, just deep enough for Jake to splash and play. As she approached, she could see sun glistening on the dark hair on Sam's chest. He made a spectacular sight sitting there playing with his son. She wished she were able to tell him that she'd never be attracted to him, but to her dismay, she knew that wasn't the case. She didn't like his hard approach to life, but that didn't keep her from appreciating his beauty, and being physically attracted to him. What an impossible position to be in.

She loved watching him with Jake. He became a different person. Which one was the real Sam du Cannon? The hard, no-nonsense business tycoon, or the warm, laughing, loving father?

As she approached them, he looked up and watched her walk toward them. His eyes traveled her entire length before coming back to hers. It was hard for her to find a bathing suit that fit the top part of her body correctly, as her breasts were much larger than average, and there was an impressive expanse of cleavage showing. The motions of swimming had worked the suit even lower than when she first put it on. Droplets of water cascaded down her cleavage to disappear in the valley below. Sam's eyes took in all of it, and he felt a stirring in the lower part of his body.

Before he could analyze his thoughts, Jake discovered Nella and ran toward her. She sat down in the water beside Sam and started playing with Jake. Soon all three of them were in a water-splashing game that had sheets of water flying everywhere, and their peals of laughter sounded like any happy little family out for a day of fun.

Friday, as Nella dressed for the company party, she felt butterflies fluttering in her stomach. She was a little nervous. Taking care of a three-year-old was one thing, but going out in public to a party, pretending to be the happy bride of a man who didn't even like her, was going to be quite another.

She was happy with the results of her efforts when she was dressed. She'd bought a beautiful purple three-piece outfit. The color was wonderful on her. The neckline of the fitted bodice dipped just low enough to show the enticing beginning of cleavage. The skirt was straight and reached just below mid-calf, and the jacket that completed the ensemble was a soft gauze-like material that flowed when she walked. She wore a long faux pearl necklace and pearl drop earrings. Her dark hair was cooperating exceptionally well, and she knew she looked her best tonight.

When Sam returned from taking Jake to the baby-sitter, Nella was ready and waiting for him. "You look very nice tonight," was all he said, but several times she felt his eyes on her as they drove to the party.

Sam looked even better than usual. He had on a black suit, yellow shirt, and a black and yellow paisley tie. The yellow shirt enhanced his dark hair and bronze complexion, and made his unusual eyes even more startling than they normally were. Nella wanted to tell him how devastatingly handsome he looked, but she was afraid she couldn't be as passive and nonchalant with her compliment as he had been with his. And she sure wasn't about to let him know just how handsome she thought he was.

She could feel excitement start deep inside her in anticipation of the challenge that lay ahead. It had been a while since she'd had a chance to go to a party, and she was anxious to get the evening under way.

When they entered the main room, Nella was surprised at the large crowd. People mingled everywhere. She had no idea Sam's company was this large. Actually, she knew nothing about his work, as they never discussed it.

Sam introduced her to several people, and then disappeared into the crowd. She tried to mingle for a while, but soon realized these people all had their own little cliques and their own common interests, and she was an outsider. She casually made her way to the bar. She was aware that eyes followed her and comments were made, but didn't trouble herself trying to second-guess what was thought or said.

She ordered a glass of champagne and leaned against the bar to sip her drink as she watched the party goers. She loved watching people as they struggled to impress each other and themselves. Especially women. She had held to a theory for a long time that women dressed for each other. Women seemed to have an obsessive desire to impress the other women around them. The competition had always been a mystery to her. Why couldn't women just enjoy who they were as individuals?

Occasionally she caught a glimpse of Sam as he drifted from group to group. He seemed well-liked and accepted among his co-workers, and the smile on his face was warm and friendly. That was the most surprising. She'd only seen that look on his face for Jake. Apparently he could be very charming. She noticed several women openly flirting with him, even though they knew he was married now.

She was brought out of her deep thoughts by a quiet voice close beside her. "What's a beautiful lady like you doing standing here alone?" The line wasn't unusual, but it brought a slight smile to Nella's lips.

The man standing beside her had startling blue eyes that seemed to be trying to pierce her soul. His hair was sandy brown and was beginning to recede at the hairline. His eyes were the only out-standing feature about his face. The light reflecting off them made them sparkle like cut glass.

Before she could answer, he reached over and took the glass from her hand and set it on the bar. "Would you allow me your first dance of the evening?"

Without saying a word, Nella allowed him to take her hand and lead her to the dance floor.

She loved playing "the games" at these social settings. She never took the comments seriously, and she had never seen a man yet she couldn't outwit in these little charades. In fact, more men than she knew had walked away feeling a little jilted when they'd had to go home alone.

The first dance was a waltz. Nella and Blue Eyes swayed with the music as if they'd danced together all their lives. She could tell he loved to dance by the way he moved and guided her through the steps. He really wasn't trying to hit on her. He just wanted to dance. Soon the waltz stopped and the band struck up a Rumba.

"Can you Rumba?" he asked.

"Try me," she said.

At times like these she was so thankful her father had started her in dance classes at an early age, and that she had loved dancing enough to continue taking classes even up to the present. There weren't many dances she couldn't do.

Her love for dancing showed now as she and her partner blended and became one with the music. He was good! How she appreciated dancing with a good partner!

She wasn't aware that the other dancers had cleared the dance floor just to stand and watch her and her partner move and sway to the sensual beat of the Rumba. She didn't hear the comments of how well she danced, and, on several occasions, how beautiful she was. She didn't see the scowl on Sam's face.

Only when the music stopped and people applauded did she realize what had taken place. She had barely caught her breath when the band started again, and another man took her hand to dance.

Thus went her evening. She only paused long enough to switch partners and then continue dancing.

She was beginning to feel tired when the band started a slower than usual waltz. She felt strong arms surround her, and a very familiar aftershave engulfed her. She looked up into Sam's golden eyes.

"My, my, aren't we just the social butterfly?" She heard the trace of sarcasm in his voice.

"Well, I've never been a wallflower, Sam. So if that makes me a social butterfly, then I guess I am. But what do you care?" She could tell he was angry, but she was at a loss as to why.

"You've danced with every man here tonight! How does that make me look?"

"No, Sam, I've danced with every man here that has asked me, except you, my new husband, who hasn't, until now, acted like he even knows me. How does *that* make you look? And when you finally do ask me to dance, you've done nothing but scowl at me. Surely, you don't think you can bring me to a party, desert me, and expect me to stand where you left me until you return?"

She was expecting anything except his lips descending and engulfing hers in a long, gentle kiss.

He had to shut her up, and it was the first thing that came to his mind. When he ended the kiss she was too stunned to say a word. He led her from the room.

Glances and smiles were exchanged as heads nodded knowingly at each other. To the people left behind, Sam and Nella looked like two lovers leaving in the heat of the moment for pleasures that couldn't wait.

As for Sam, he wondered what in the hell had just happened.

And for Nella? She smiled softly to herself, knowing she had just won another argument.

After the car was in motion toward the hotel, Nella broke the silence. "Sam, who is John McHill?"

"I've known John for years. He and his dates used to double date with Vanessa and me. Why?" His voice was tense from the remembered kiss.

"He was asking me a lot of questions about you and me and Jake. He mentioned Jake's grandparents wanting to raise him so badly. How does he know about that? Have you told him?"

"Everybody at the office knows I'm having to fight them to keep Jake, so the word probably got to John somehow. I've never spoken to him directly about the situation. I don't see him as much as I used to, now that Vanessa is gone."

"Well," and her voice became more concerned, "I don't like him. I don't trust him, and I felt like he was interrogating me. I felt like he only asked me to dance so he could ask me questions. I think you need to be very careful around him."

"I think maybe you're overreacting, but I'll watch for any strange actions from him."

"Oh." She couldn't resist telling him the next thing. "He said he found it strange that you'd married a plus-sized woman. He said he was the one who went for the full-figured women, and you always wanted the string beans."

Sam didn't bother to comment. They rode in silence for a few minutes, then he asked, "Who was your blue-eyed dance partner? Someone you know?"

"This was your company party, Sam. How am I supposed to know him? Don't you know him?"

"No, I don't know who he is."

"Then he must have come with one of your employees, because I sure don't know who he is."

"Well, he sure seemed to want to know you better. You two were quite a spectacle on the dance floor."

"In what way? Did I embarrass you?"

"No. In fact, you're a very graceful dancer. Half the men there were drooling over you."

"Is that a bad thing?" Under any other circumstance Nella would have thought he was jealous, but she knew Sam du Cannon wasn't jealous of other men looking at her.

"Let's just drop it, okay?"

They finished the drive in silence. Nella, smiling, remembering how much fun the evening had been, and, Sam, wishing he could stop seeing Nella's body swaying to that sizzling Latin music, and feeling those full, warm lips yielding beneath his.

Chapter 4

Nella left Jake at the hotel's childcare center and spent part of the day shopping. She needed some time alone for a change. It'd been a week since the company party, and she was still on a high from the good time she'd had. Sam had been a little distant for a couple of days after the party, but soon things had settled back into their previous routine.

She bought a couple of items, but mostly just browsed and relaxed.

When she returned to get Jake, she had to wait for the mother ahead of her to get her two little boys, ages approximately two and four, who ran to their mother calling, "Mommy, Mommy!"

Nella watched Jake as he stood quietly and absorbed the transactions between mother and children. She wondered what he was thinking, and he was unusually quiet on the way home.

She forgot the incident until later that night.

They had finished dinner and Nella was stacking the dishes in the dishwasher. Jake sat on Sam's lap and listened intently to the story Sam was reading to him. When the story ended, Jake sat quietly for a few minutes, instead of running and putting the book away as he usually did. Suddenly he sat up and looked Sam directly in the eyes.

"Nella's my mommy now, okay?"

Nella froze in her tracks as her eyes met Sam's across Jake's head. She watched several emotions pass over Sam's face as they stared at each other.

Jake reached up and with a hand on each side of Sam's face, pulled his father's head down to make his dad look him in the eyes. "And now I'll call her Mommy, okay?"

"Jake," Sam's voice was quiet and gentle. "Will you go to your room and let Nella and me discuss this?"

The child climbed from his father's lap and obediently started for the door to his room. Just before he got to the door, he stopped and turned back to his father. He pointed his finger at Sam and in a very serious voice said, "You better say yes!" Then he entered his room and closed the door.

Disbelief registered on both the adults' faces before they broke into uncontrollable laughter. They tried to muffle their voices so Jake couldn't hear, but they didn't succeed very well.

Finally gaining control, Sam asked, "Where on earth did *that* come from?"

"I guess being at the childcare center has taught him more than to share his toys," Nella answered, wiping tears from her eyes and sitting down in the nearest chair.

They both realized they had a question to resolve.

"So, what do you think?" he asked, watching her intently.

Nella couldn't believe Sam du Cannon was actually asking her opinion on the matter. She figured he'd be totally against it. He sensed her surprise, but continued.

"You show an uncanny ability to know what's best for my son. I watch with growing amazement as you teach him good manners, good, sound health habits, and a lot of other things that I would never even think about teaching a child his age. I've watched him settle down and become secure in his life with you. So, yes, to my own surprise, I'm asking what do you think is best for this situation?"

"Sam," she said, in the soft throaty voice he was beginning to look forward to hearing, "I honestly don't know. And you apparently aren't sure, so let's leave it up to Jake. He might call me Mommy for a few days, and then drop it. I'm sure it's because he's heard the kids at the daycare greet their mothers, calling them Mommy."

"So you don't mind being called Mommy?"

"Well, it obviously will take some getting used to, but no, I don't mind."

"Then let's call Jake and discuss this with him. Jake, come here, please," Sam called.

The door opened and the child came hesitantly into the room. The previous spontaneous, demanding attitude was gone now as he timidly awaited his answer.

"Come here, Son." Sam lifted him to his lap. "Why do you want to call Nella Mommy?"

"Because she is!" This was said as if anyone should be able to understand it.

"You know she's not your real mommy. You remember your real mommy, don't you?"

Nella was always amazed at the love and tenderness Sam used when he addressed his son.

"Yes, I bemember my 'nother mommy. But she's not here now, and Nella is." Such simple logic could only come from a child.

"Yes, Jake, Nella is here now. And I know you love her, and she loves you. We discussed it, and she doesn't mind, and I don't mind, if you call her Mommy."

"So it's okay?" The little boy almost seemed afraid to hope.

"Yes, it's okay," Sam answered.

Jake slid off Sam's lap and stood looking at Nella for a brief moment, then started running around the room in circles, whooping and chanting, "Mommy, Mommy, I've got a Mommy!"

Emotions overwhelmed Nella, and tears unashamedly poured down her face. She knew she would go through whatever it took to be a mother to this child. At this moment he was truly hers. She might not have given birth to him, but she could give him a life he'd always remember and cherish. She would be the mother to him that she had always longed to have. She was suddenly filled with joy and commitment.

She looked at Sam and found him watching her intently. His face was also moist with tears. He cleared his throat, but his voice was gruff with emotion as he spoke. "I didn't know a woman like you existed."

The light in his eyes had never been directed toward her, and it took her by such surprise that she felt as if her heart would explode in her chest. Their eyes locked across the room, and nothing seemed to exist but the two of them. At that moment Jake, still doing his celebration dance, came flying into her lap and smacked her bottom lip with his forehead.

As her lip was caught between his head and her teeth she cried out in pain, blood immediately running down her chin.

"Jake! Settle down, now!" Sam admonished the excited child.

Astonishment filled the little boy's eyes as he watched Nella try to blot the blood with her hand, only to smear it on her chin.

"Oh, Mommy, I'm so sorry." His voice was hushed as he patted her face with his small hands.

Nella was in too much pain to reassure him at that point. Suddenly Sam was beside her with a cold, wet bath cloth. He lifted Jake from her lap and gently placed the cloth on her broken lip.

There was a warm glow in his eyes as he asked, "Are you really sure about this?"

"I've never been more sure about anything in my life," she answered around the cold cloth and her rapidly swelling bottom lip.

The next morning, Sam called from the office to tell her some of the office crew were having a spur-of-the-moment beach party, and could she and Jake be ready to go by eight o'clock that evening.

Nella tried to beg off, but Sam insisted that it was a family outing, and Jake would love it. She'd finally given in without too much argument, but now she wasn't so sure.

The group had found a calypso band that would play for them, and the music was fairly good. Nella hadn't come prepared for a swimming party, but several of the children were splashing around in the water, and Jake was begging to go in with them.

She'd worn a white cotton dress with a red belt, red necklace and earrings, and red sandals. She couldn't wade in with Jake and let him play because the salt water would turn her white dress an ugly yellow. She wished she and Sam had discussed this "outing" a little more thoroughly, so she could have been better prepared for Jake to enjoy it.

The wind was causing the water to be rough tonight. The air was balmier than usual, it seemed, but the moon was beautiful, and glistened on the water each time a wave rippled.

"Can I please, please, please go in the water?" Jake begged.

Nella was not comfortable with him being in the water as rough as it was, but she hated for him to feel left out. She looked around, trying to find the solution to her problem. She took Jake by the hand and led him toward the nearby fishing pier. A few people sat on the pier, talking and enjoying the music and the evening.

Soon she found a piece of rope that had been left behind by a fisherman. She picked it up with no plan in mind, but hoping some brilliant idea would strike her at any moment.

A couple of the women from the office party were standing around talking. As she and Jake walked by, they heard him begging to play in the water.

"Jake, Sweetheart, I'm trying to figure something out for you, just give me a moment."

"Mrs. du Cannon?" Nella almost walked on by, not immediately responding to the name she wasn't used to.

"Mrs. du Cannon?" the voice repeated.

"Yes?" Nella stopped.

"I don't know if you remember me. I'm Jan, and this is Sue." She indicated her friend.

"Yes," Nella acknowledged. "I remember you both. How are you tonight?"

"Oh, having a great time! Look, I don't mean to interfere, but I heard your son asking to go swimming. I brought an extra life jacket in case one of Amy's friends needed it. You're welcome to use it if you want to."

"Thanks, but I'm afraid for Jake to be in the water as rough as it is. I'm afraid he might drift too far out." She casually fingered the rope she was still holding. Then the idea came to her. "On second thought, I *will* borrow the life jacket, if you don't mind."

Jake immediately started jumping up and down with happiness.

She went back to where the other children were, and, looking around, found a fold-up chair no one was using. She put the life jacket on Jake, then tied the rope onto one of the belt loops of the life jacket, making sure there was no way it could come untied. Then she formed a loop in the other end and placed her chair leg over the loop. She made sure Jake was close enough to play with the other children, but not close enough that one of them could get tangled in the rope.

She leaned back in the chair and smiled. Now Jake was happy, and she could sit here and listen to the music and the ocean and relax a little.

"That plan would make MacGyver envious."

Nella jumped at the closeness of the voice. John McHill stood so near, he was almost brushing up against her.

"Thank you," she acknowledged, glancing at Jake. He was totally happy now, splashing around with the other children. A wave lifted him occasionally, and he laughed with glee as he rode it down.

"He's a fine boy." Again, the voice interrupted her thoughts.

"Yes, he is." Nella smiled, her pride in the child obvious.

"Too bad his real mother won't be able to watch him grow up." Was there a touch of sarcasm in his softly spoken words?

"Yes, it's a shame," Nella agreed. She didn't want to get into a conversation with this man, but at the same time she didn't want to be rude, as Sam had indicated he'd been friends with John for some time.

Now the man took her hand in his and leaned down to her.

"Nella, what are you doing with Sam du Cannon? You're not his type. Is this marriage just to throw his in-laws off track?" His face was so close to Nella's she could smell the garlic on his breath.

"Get out of my face!" She was instantly angry. She couldn't get up because he was so close, but she couldn't get up anyway, since she had to stay seated to keep Jake's rope anchored.

"Does he make love to you? Not like I would. I'd love to get you in bed!"

"If you don't leave me alone," she ground out between clenched teeth, "I'm going to scream rape."

His chuckle was nasty. "Baby, it wouldn't be rape. You'd love every minute of it. If you change your mind, you let me know!" And he turned and walked away.

During her exchange with him she had been vaguely aware of a child's voice calling "Mommy, Mommy!" repeatedly. Now, she heard it again, more faintly. That reminded her of Jake, and she glanced to make sure he was okay.

Where was he?

"Jake!" she screamed.

Then she saw the small object bobbing in the distance. Instinctively she knew it was Jake. She saw the loose end of the rope floating in the water.

In one fluid move she was out of her shoes and dress and into the water. She started swimming toward the child in swift, strong movements.

How had this happened? She *knew* the rope was secure enough! Had one of the other kids untied it? No! She'd tied it in several knots! Had that been Jake calling her all the time? She knew it'd been him. Poor little guy. He was probably scared to death, and she hadn't responded to his cries for help.

But she wasn't used to being called Mommy, so in her angry dispute with John McHill it hadn't registered on her that she was being called. Anyway, she would have bet her own life there was no way that rope could have come undone.

She was beginning to feel tired. She raised her head occasionally to check on her progress toward the small bobbing object that seemed to be drifting away from her faster than she was swimming. Was she getting any closer to him? The waves seemed to be getting larger now, and rougher.

Oh, God, she pleaded mentally. She couldn't lose this child! She had to reach him.

Her lungs were beginning to hurt. *I must not panic!* With sheer force of effort and self-control, she made herself concentrate on her breathing.

Suddenly the moon went behind a cloud, and she felt the wind pick up. She couldn't see anything.

"NO!" Did she actually scream out loud, or just in her inner being? It was going to storm! She could feel it in the air now. In fact, she'd felt it in the air all evening. All the signs had been there.

She dog paddled in circles, trying to tread water and find Jake. Just then the moon slid from behind the cloud long enough for Nella to see him being lifted on a huge wave.

In awe, she watched. There was nothing she could do. Then she realized the wave and the child were rolling straight toward her.

Struggling to keep her head above the churning water, she watched as the child came rapidly toward her. If she didn't catch him, the rolling wave would take him under and he would drown.

As he came closer and Nella waited, she realized he was too far to the right. She was going to lose him. He was going to go right by her, and she would never find him. She could tell he was crying.

Then she saw the rope flopping around on the churning water. Could she reach it? She gave a tremendous kick, using all the strength she could muster, and grabbed at the rope. She felt her fingertips brush it, but it slipped through her grasp. Frantically, she kept flailing and struggling until she again felt the rope. Desperately she grabbed at it, and this time she caught it. She held on with sheer determination, then, pulling the rope hand over hand, she drew Jake to her.

Instinctively, she popped her hand over his mouth and nose just as the wave took them under.

She felt as if she were being thrust to the bottom of the ocean. Her lungs were crushing with pressure. Jake was struggling now, needing air — desperately needing to breathe.

She kept kicking her feet and pumping with the arm that wasn't holding Jake to her body. Was she going up or down? She couldn't tell anymore.

Just when she thought she wouldn't be able to hold her breath any longer, her head popped out of the water.

Gasping great gulps of air, she lifted Jake out of the water. He was coughing and choking spasmodically. Finally he lay limp against her shoulder. She tried to ask him if he was okay, but her voice wouldn't come.

Too exhausted to even think, she started struggling toward the lights she could see in the far distance. Lights that were quickly drawing closer and closer. Was she swimming that fast? Then she heard the sound of the motor, and realized a boat was approaching. They would be rescued!

Relief flooded through her, and soon she felt herself being pulled from the water.

Nella slowly opened her eyes. She was in a bed in a dimly lit room. But where? This wasn't the hotel suite. Then she saw the nurse.

"Where am I?" she whispered weakly.

The nurse turned and came to her. "Well, it's about time you woke up."

"Why am I in a hospital?" she asked, still woozy, but needing an answer.

"The doctor can explain in the morning. You just go back to sleep, now, and get your rest."

Nella wanted to argue, but the idea of sleep sounded so good she decided she'd wait until tomorrow to argue with the nurse. Then suddenly her eyes popped open and she tried to sit up. The nurse caught her shoulders.

"Where's Jake?" The question was desperate, and demanded an answer.

"He's at home with his father. He's fine, thanks to you." The nurse lowered Nella back on the pillow, and patted her face. "You did a very brave thing when you saved that little boy's life."

Nella smiled as tears ran down her face. Jake was safe! She fell instantly asleep.

But she was restless the rest of the night. Several times she awoke abruptly, thinking a bright light had flashed in her eyes. But the room was always dimly lit, and the only noise was the soft stirrings of the nurses in the hallway.

She came slowly awake the next morning to the sound of hushed male voices.

A doctor was talking, and Nella strained to hear what he was saying. "Your wife is one of the healthiest people I've ever examined," he softly told Sam. "If one single thing had been different about her, you would have lost her and your son. And if everybody were as healthy as she is, I'd have to sit and wait for an accident to happen, just so I'd have work to do. I don't know what she does to stay in shape, but she could teach us all a few things."

Sam was about to comment when he looked toward her and realized she was awake. She wished she could have heard the beginning of their conversation.

"Well, good morning!" The doctor spoke first, coming toward her. "How do you feel?"

"I want to go home." Her voice was still weak, but she could feel it getting stronger.

"Well, I think we can arrange that," the doctor said, turning to the nurse at the foot of her bed.

"Blood pressure?" he inquired.

"110 over 70." She read the chart.

"Pulse rate?"

"70."

"Temperature?"

"Normal."

He smiled and took Nella's hand. "You did a remarkable thing last night, Mrs. du Cannon. But you were very close to exhaustion when they brought you in. You still had some water in your lungs, so we kept you overnight. You're fine now, and you can go home. It's been my pleasure to be able to look after you." He patted her on the shoulder, turned and shook Sam's hand, then left the room.

It only took fifteen minutes to get from the hospital to the hotel suite. Nella was so busy trying to put the pieces of the puzzle together that she was grateful Sam didn't talk. How did that rope come untied? She knew Sam was furious with her for doing such a stupid thing in the first place. He'd probably call the whole marriage off now. She'd lose Jake forever.

Silently, Sam helped her get up to their suite. Then he went to the daycare center and got Jake.

She was leaning back on the couch with her eyes closed when she heard them returning. She was not prepared for the charge of emotion that hit her when the small boy burst through the door and ran to her.

"I missed you, Nel — Mommy!" he exclaimed, crawling onto her lap and wrapping his arms tightly around her neck.

Nella couldn't say a word. She held the precious body close to hers and wept quietly. Soon he pulled away from her and looked at her in concern. "Does it hurt somewhere?" he asked, and patted her face.

"No, Son." Two strong hands lifted him from her lap. "Nella doesn't hurt anywhere, she's just happy to know you're okay. Now I want you to go get on your bed and rest for a little while. I need to talk with Nella."

"But she needs to hold me," his voice quivered. He was becoming upset at seeing Nella cry.

"She can hold you as long as you want when we finish talking, okay?"

The promise seemed to be fairly satisfactory to the child, and he reluctantly left the room.

Nella regained control, and dabbed at her eyes with the tissue Sam handed her. She mentally braced herself for what was coming. When she finally looked up, Sam sat quietly watching her. The fury she expected was not in evidence on his face. Instead, he handed her a newspaper.

Questioningly, she took it and looked down at the front page.

A gasp of disbelief escaped her as she gazed at a full-page photo of herself wearing only a bra, panties, a red necklace and red earrings. She was obviously soaked and quite dazed-looking.

"What — is — this?" she choked out.

"That's you, right after we pulled you out of the water."

"But who would take a picture of me like that?" Disbelief was giving way to agitation.

"The press, obviously." His voice had not changed tones. He spoke quietly and in control. Nella wondered when the explosion would hit.

"Read the caption," he instructed.

She read,

Nobody's Perfect

Food tycoon Sam du Cannon almost lost his only son last night due to the carelessness of his party-loving wife.

She stared at him through huge, tear-filled eyes.

"Oh, Sam. I'm so sorry. I know it was stupid of me to take a chance like that, but I would have bet my life that rope would never come untied! Do you want me to leave? I — "

He held his hands up to stop her. "Nella — Nella! The rope didn't come untied."

She stared at him opened-mouthed as he answered her unasked question.

"It was cut."

Chapter 5

"Cut? But how? Who would do such a thing? Did one of the other kids have a sharp object in the water?" She would have gone on, but again, Sam stopped her.

"Nella, the rope was cut just below the chair leg. In fact, one of the policemen suggested that you did it. They wanted to question you."

She felt dead inside. Did Sam believe she'd do something like that?

"Sam, if I had cut that rope, would I have risked my life trying to save Jake?"

"That's exactly what I asked the authorities." His answer was quiet and reassuring. "That's when they realized they were making a wrong assumption."

"Then they're not going to question me?" Hope was again creeping into her voice.

"Well, they want to talk to you. Nella, someone was close enough to you to cut that rope, if you were in that chair the whole time."

Suddenly John McHill's leering face came to her.

"John McHill," she almost whispered.

"I told you John was a friend of mine." Sam's voice was impatient.

"Then why did he proposition your wife last night, if he's your friend?"

"*Whaat?*" Disbelief resounded in his voice. "What did he say to you?"

"Sam — " Nella hesitated. "What he said isn't important. He just made some cheap, low-class remarks." She didn't want to repeat the things John had said.

"Don't you think I have the right to know if someone is coming on to my wife?" Sam's eyes bored into Nella's. A stunned silence settled over the room as they both realized how easily and naturally he had used the term "wife."

Nella got slowly to her feet. The press? How did the press get there that fast? Did someone call them and tell them a rescue was in progress?

Missing pieces were falling into place. The flashes she had kept seeing during the night were memory replays of the cameras going off around her. But something else was bothering her. John McHill had something in his hand when he was talking to her. Was it a drink? No. He had been doing something when she first looked up. But what? She had to remember!

She pressed her fingers against her temples as she stood and gazed out the window. Someone walking on the beach far below her stooped and picked up a piece of driftwood —

"Whittling!" she almost shouted, as she turned back to Sam.

"What are you talking about?" Sam asked, his mind still on the previous subject.

"John was whittling a piece of driftwood when he first walked up to me last night." Realization dawned on her face. "He must have said those things to startle me so much that I wouldn't pay attention to what he was doing."

"That's a very strong accusation." Sam still sounded unconvinced. "But," he added, as if talking himself, "it was John who showed up with the boat we used to rescue you. And come to think of it, the press was with him. He said they'd been covering a party down the beach when they heard the commotion."

"But why? What does this mean?"

"It means, I'm guessing, that you fouled up a heroic rescue he had planned."

"I don't understand."

"Don't you see? He must be involved with my in-laws. He cut Jake loose so he could rescue him and make me look like an incompetent parent. But you jumped in and saved Jake, so he had to turn the picture on you, no pun intended. The press had to have already been called. There's no way they could have gotten there that fast. It was all a set-up." Again Sam was holding the paper. "That's why this article is so slanted against you. Will you be okay for a while? Do you feel strong enough to cope with Jake?"

"I'm fine," she said. She wanted to ask him where he was going, but decided against it.

Sam locked the door behind him as he left, and Nella went in search of Jake. He was in the middle of his bed, curled up in a small bundle, sound asleep.

He looked so tiny lying there. Tears filled her eyes again as she thought of how close she had come to losing him.

John McHill may have thought his plan was foolproof, but he couldn't have known there would be a storm. His staged rescue had almost turned tragic.

She lay down on the bed and pulled the small bundle close to her. He sighed
deeply and snuggled closer. Holding him tightly, Nella soon slept.

That's how Sam found them two and a half hours later. Neither had moved, still exhausted from the night before.

As he watched them lying there, Nella holding Jake close and protected against her, he felt something stirring deep inside. An emotion that was new to him. An emotion he wasn't ready to identify.

Nella came awake to voices in the living room. Jake was no longer beside her. Was it the police? Had they come to question her? She glanced at her watch. Six o'clock! She'd slept for four hours!

Slowly she got up and straightened her hair and clothes before starting to the living room. Sam was saying good-bye to someone at the door.

Jake saw her first and came to give her a big hug. "You slept for a long time, Mommy. Daddy and me had to be real quiet so we didn't wake you up." A warm ray of pleasure shot through her, just knowing Sam had made a special effort to let her rest. She was gradually changing her opinion of him. He really wasn't as hard a man as she had thought at first.

Sam turned from the door and motioned toward the dining table. "That was room service. I thought we all needed a good hot meal, but I didn't think you'd feel like going out. Jake ordered for you."

She couldn't believe all the food that was spread on the table before her. Jake was on his knees in one of the chairs, leaning on the table with his elbows, surveying the food.

"That looks like a lot of fat gwams to me," he said solemnly.

Laughter exploded from Sam. When he caught his breath, he asked, "What are you teaching my son?"

"I'm trying to teach him how to eat so he'll always be healthy," she said. "And it wouldn't hurt you to pay some attention, yourself. Jake," she continued, "why is it important for us to watch our fat grams?"

"So we can have a healthy car — cardoorvaslalar sistern," he finished, looking important that he had said such a large word.

"That's right, Son!" Sam exclaimed, lifting Jake from the chair and high above his head. "And I'm very impressed with you for knowing such a good word. What is your cardiovascular system?"

"It's your heart, Daddy. Eberybody knows that."

After the laughter had quieted down, Sam turned to Nella, looking very serious.

"I'm being forced to be impressed with you," he admitted honestly. "The doctor said you were one of the healthiest people he'd ever seen. Some time ago I accused you of eating to try to impress me. And, I admit, I thought you were probably just going down and lying on the beach every morning instead of swimming, but now I know how wrong I've been. If you weren't really doing all the things you seem to be doing, you could never have saved Jake's life last night. I apologize for misjudging you, and I really appreciate what you're doing with my son. And I don't even know how to thank you for saving him last night." Emotions choked Sam's voice down to a gruff whisper.

Tears filled Nella's eyes as she reached out and briefly squeezed Sam's hand. "I can't imagine a mother who wouldn't risk her life for her child," Nella said, looking deeply into Sam's eyes.

The next morning when Nella got up, Sam had already left.

She went to the kitchen, poured a cup of coffee, and reached for the morning paper. The headlines jumped out at her. There was another full-page cover story about her. But this time it was an apology, and a full, correct account of how she had rescued her stepson, with much praise for her and her heroic actions.

She shook her head in amazement. Sam du Cannon must be a very powerful man to be able to convince the press to eat crow. That must have been where he went when he left yesterday.

She would have loved to have seen him in action. She gave a slight shudder, imagining how he could be if he were really angry.

She had barely gotten dressed when she heard someone knocking on the door. She opened it to find two policemen standing in front of her.

"Yes?" she asked, but knowing why they were there.

"Ma'am, we hate to bother you, but we need to ask you some questions about what happened the other night."

Nella was dismayed. She didn't think she'd be questioned now that everyone knew she couldn't have been involved with what had happened.

"Why do you want to question me?" she asked. The two officers were very young and couldn't have been out of the academy very long.

"Well, ma'am, you know that rope was cut, and we have to try to find out who did it. May we come in?"

"You certainly may not!" Sam was close behind the two officers, and they hadn't seen him come up. They both jumped at his loud interjection.

"You boys need to check with Chief Carlson before you try to start questioning my wife. This case is closed as far as she's concerned. Maybe you two need to go direct traffic somewhere." Sam's eyes were cold as he stepped past the two officers and closed the door behind him.

"I am so glad you came when you did. I didn't know what to do." Relief flooded through Nella.

"You are in no way to be questioned about what happened. If something like that happens again, you call this man." Sam handed Nella a business card. "This is my lawyer, Dan Beasly. Just tell him you're my wife, and he'll tell you what to do. I don't think it'll happen again after I call Chief Carlson, but you keep that card anyway. Call Dan if you ever get into a situation where you need advice."

As Sam finished his sentence, he picked up the phone and dialed a number. "Chief Carlson, this is Sam du Cannon. Two of your overeager young upstarts were here just now, trying to question my wife about the incident the other night. I would appreciate it if that doesn't happen again."

Nella watched as Sam made the call. He was the embodiment of strength. She felt a thrill of excitement just watching him. He looked up and caught her eyes, and winked.

Her pulse leaped. She made a hasty retreat to look out the window. Surely she wasn't about to blush! But her face sure felt like it was turning red. She must really be tired, to be acting like a silly schoolgirl.

Sam's laughter brought her back to his conversation. "Yes, I do think a little traffic duty would bring them back down to earth. Thanks, again, Chief." He hung up the phone.

"I don't think you'll have any more problems," Sam assured her.

Chapter 6

The sunset was so beautiful that Nella felt a lump rise to her throat as she sat on the beach, alone, and watched the sun sink slowly behind the horizon.

She reflected over the past two months. The two months of her marriage. She still had to stop occasionally and ask herself where she was and what was really happening.

She had left Jake at the daycare center and strolled along the beach for a long time. She needed to be alone today, just to think, just to meditate, just to try to take mental stock of what was happening to her life. Sam had called to say he had a late meeting and would not be home before eight-thirty or nine o'clock, so she had decided to get out for a little while.

She stopped in the shade of a large sand dune to watch the spectacular sunset. She was so engrossed in the colorful sky that the voices of the approaching couple were very close to her before she realized anyone was near.

The couple stopped just before they reached the sand dune concealing her from their view. Their conversation drifted over to Nella.

The all-too-familiar voice of her husband came through the softening twilight. "Miranda, I can't afford to take a chance like that."

"But Sam — " The voice was soft and persuasive. "We were so close before you got married. I miss the times we spent together. I miss being in your arms."

Nella knew she should speak up and let them know she was there, but she sat spellbound, remembering the name and voice as belonging to a shapely blonde she'd met at the company party. So this was Sam's late office meeting. Was this what he was doing every time he said he was working late?

"I know we had some good times, but I have enemies that are watching my every move, and they won't miss a chance to slap an adultery charge on me, proving me to be an unfit parent. If they caught me going out with you, or if it even looked like I was dating you, that's all they'd need to have me back in court."

"Are you sure that's what's stopping you? Maybe you really are in love with your wife." The bitter tone of a jilted woman crept into her voice. "I saw how you were looking at her at the company party, and you sure looked like a jealous husband to me. I don't think you liked seeing her dance with all those other men."

"Miranda, don't be ridiculous! You're just grabbing at straws now." Sam's tone of voice was becoming impatient.

"But Sam, she's fat. You deserve better than that!" Her voice was whining now.

"Miranda, you've said quite enough!" The sharpness of his voice surprised Nella. "Nella," he continued, "is turning out to be the biggest surprise of my life. I never knew that a woman of her character existed, and her size has nothing to do with anything you and I need to discuss."

"My word! You *are* in love with her!" There was genuine shock in her voice.

"And the full moon is getting to you. Come on, I'm taking you home." Sam's voice faded as they walked back in the opposite direction.

Nella became aware that as she sat and listened to the conversation the sun had set, and a full moon was, indeed, beginning to light up the sky. She got up and slowly made her way toward the hotel.

So Sam and Miranda had been lovers. Did he love Miranda? Surely he would have shown more emotion tonight if he did. She couldn't believe he had actually defended her to the woman he had recently been having an affair with. Especially since he'd said he would never be attracted to her. Was he possibly changing his mind?

No. She was sure his stand had been only to protect Jake.

As she reached for the daycare's door it opened suddenly to reveal Sam with Jake in his arms. The glare he gave her made her wonder briefly if he knew she'd eavesdropped on him and Miranda.

He didn't say a word as he turned and started toward the elevator. Not knowing what to expect, she followed him inside just as the elevator doors slid closed.

She didn't realize that her hair was thoroughly tousled from her hours on the beach, and that her smoky blue eyes looked questioning and mysterious from her newfound knowledge of him. She didn't know, as he stood and glared at her, that he was thinking how beautiful she looked standing in front of him.

He unlocked the door and had barely stepped inside before he turned on her and asked, "Where were you?" His tone was mildly accusing, and set Nella immediately on the defensive.

"Out," she stated flatly, as she brushed past him to go to the living room.

"With whom?" Now his voice was low and very accusing. Nella could not believe this was happening. She couldn't tell him too much, or he'd suspect her of knowing where he was tonight.

"I just went for a stroll on the beach." She kept her voice quiet and honest.

"Where?" She saw the glint in his golden eyes.

"Up around Morgan's Bend," she lied, as she'd been in the opposite direction.

"And were you alone? You weren't with any of your admirers from the party?"

"Well, my, my, Sam. I never took you for the jealous type." She smiled coyly at him. She had to try to throw him off track before he found out where she'd really been.

"I just can't afford any more media exposure right now," he said, standing and looking out the window. In a few minutes, he turned back to her. "Pack the bags. We're leaving tomorrow as soon as I can book a flight."

"Why are we leaving here?" she asked, already knowing. But she wondered if he was running from potential publicity, or from his feelings for Miranda.

"I just think it's time to get away from everyone for awhile. This situation with John McHill lets me know my in-laws are trying harder than ever to get their hands on Jake. We need to disappear for a while."

"Disappear? Where?" Nella didn't think she liked the mysterious sound of that word.

"To my grandparents' home in Kentucky. That's where I go when I need time to think."

"Do they know we're coming?"

"Actually, they've both been dead for several years and the place is mine, but I always think of it as theirs."

Their final flight landed in Bowling Green, Kentucky, where they went immediately to the Jeep Sam kept in storage at the airport. Everyone working at the airport seemed to know Sam. He greeted them all, and introduced Nella and Jake.

On the drive out of town Sam explained that his grandparents had raised him after his parents were killed in a plane crash when he was five years old. His grandparents were more like real parents to him than grandparents. His grandfather had worked at the airport doing odd jobs during the winter months when the farm wasn't productive.

As they drove, and Sam talked, Nella was growing more concerned at the route they were taking. Each turn they made seemed to be on to a smaller road, until finally they turned onto a dirt road that was barely wide enough for two vehicles to pass. They seemed to be gradually climbing and continuously winding around small, narrow, sharp curves and corners. Trees and foliage met overhead in places, creating a tunnel for them to pass through. Occasionally they passed a farmhouse nestled back against a protective steep hill, or saw smoke curling gently from a clump of trees, indicating that a house was there somewhere.

It was late October, and the fall colors were blazing and beautiful. The higher they climbed, the cooler the air became. A wonderful woodsy scent permeated the air, causing Nella to want to breathe deeply and inhale the glorious aroma.

Sam seemed strangely quiet. It was almost as if they were entering sacred ground and he didn't want to disturb the sleeping memories that lay in any direction he looked.

Jake had fallen asleep in his car seat. Nella was about to ask Sam how much further when the Jeep turned into a rutted driveway that showed little signs of recent use. They rounded several tight curves, still climbing, then there before them stood a huge house.

"My grandparents' place," Sam said, waving his hands in a wide sweep, indicating everything the eye could see.

Nella glanced around, but her eyes came back to the house. "Sam, this house is huge!" Her voice was hushed with awe.

"Yes. Three stories and a basement."

"What on earth did your grandparents need with a house this size if your father was an only child?"

"Yes, Dad was an only child, but their dream, when they built the house, was to fill it up with children. They wanted at least ten. But when my grandmother gave birth to my father, there was some internal damage done, and she couldn't have any more children."

Now, two weeks later, as Nella stood and watched Sam push Jake in the swing Sam had played on as a child, she wondered if she would ever have children of her own. This would be a wonderful house to raise children in.

The outside of the house fascinated, yet frightened, Nella. The house was built on a mountain, with the back overlooking a magnificent valley. But a few hundred yards from the rear of the house was an extreme bluff that went straight down, with a river running at the bottom.

She knew she'd have nightmares of Jake falling off that bluff. She'd persuade Sam to build a fence around the house so she wouldn't worry so much.

After just a few days of the new setting, Nella began to be aware of some dramatic changes taking place in Sam. She watched all the signs of stress start to slowly disappear. He was relaxed and easygoing, with none of the abruptness and impatience that had characterized him when they had first met, and while they were in Hawaii. He was up early each morning having coffee. There wasn't a paper to read, but he didn't seem to mind. He just took one of the guns out of the gun case in the hallway, and disappeared for a couple of hours each morning.

The first morning he did that, Nella was watching with a questioning look in her eyes. Just before he'd walked out the door he'd turned back and said, "Woman, I'm a-goin' a-huntin.'"

The whistle of the teakettle brought her back to the present. She made a cup of herbal tea and went outside to sit on the porch swing and watch Jake and Sam. She noticed a nip in the air as she sat down. Cold weather would soon be here, and she wondered how long Sam planned to stay.

Sam and Jake made a perfect picture of contentment as Sam pushed Jake back and forth in the swing. Jake squealed each time the swing went into the air. Soon Sam looked up and spotted Nella watching them from the porch. He waved and said something to Jake. Jake looked around at Nella and waved, and would have fallen if Sam hadn't caught him. The near fall frightened Jake, and he decided he didn't want to "sving" any more right now, so they joined Nella on the porch.

Sam slumped down in the porch swing beside Nella and rested his arm on the back of the swing behind her, surprising her with the gesture of relaxed companionship. "Nella, I believe I could spend the rest of my life here and never miss the city life." He closed his eyes and leaned his head back in contentment.

Nella was close enough to smell his outdoor scent. His shirt was open at the neck, allowing a sprinkling of chest hair to escape. His hair was tousled from being in the wind, and playing with Jake.

She had fought many urges to touch him when she found herself near him. Her most natural impulse was to reach out and touch people. Especially people she felt close to. This time she didn't fight the impulse. She leaned over and lightly kissed his cheek.

"Then why don't you?" Surprised, he opened his eyes and looked deeply into Nella's.

"Why don't I what?" His uplifted eyebrows teased Nella.

"Why don't you spend your life here? You've seemed so happy since we've been here."

He was still holding her gaze when he slowly answered, as if only just making the discovery as he spoke. "It's not just being here that's made me happy. It's being here with you and Jake. When I was growing up here, I loved it. There was always something new to do. A new place to explore, a new tree to climb, always some challenge." His arm was still on the swing behind Nella, but as he relaxed, his fingers gently brushed her back as he talked.

"Then," he continued, "when I got into high school and needed more social action, I became bored with my life here. I moved into Bowling Green so I could be where the action was. I couldn't understand how my grandparents could be so content here, but now, I'm beginning to understand." He was about to continue when Jake's excited voice interrupted him.

"Mommy! Daddy! Look, a snake!"

They both leaped from the porch swing at the same time and rushed to Jake, who stood holding a long earthworm in his hands. Relieved that it wasn't actually a snake, they both broke into laughter.

Offended that he was being laughed at, Jake threw the worm to the ground and attempted to stamp off, but Sam's long arm reached out and grabbed him. Kneeling beside Jake, Sam patiently explained what kind of worm he had, then cautioned him to never pick up something if he thought it was a snake.

After settling the matter with Jake, Nella brought up a subject that had been on her mind. "Sam, I need a place to walk. I've always been close to the beach, but I don't know anything about the woods. Is it safe for me to go in there?" She motioned toward the trees and undergrowth surrounding them.

"How far do you want to walk?"

"I need at least two miles, three or four times a week. Sometimes I go every day."

Sam was watching her intently as she talked, and when she had finished, he reached out and gently touched her face with the back of his fingers. Nella felt a tingle go up her spine, caused by the light sprinkling of hair that grew on the back of his fingers.

"You're such a good education for me. I never knew how screwed up my thinking was about f — uh, b — uh — "

Nella watched him struggle with the correct term. Two months ago he wouldn't even have tried to find a correct term; he would have just spit out the first thing that came to mind. But two months ago, he wouldn't have touched her cheek like he just did, and two months ago, her entire body wouldn't have gone weak, even if he had.

"Help me here, Nella. What is the correct term or word that I'm searching for?"

Seeing Sam du Cannon at a loss for words was an unusual sight, and Nella burst into laughter.

"Well, there are several," she said, pretending to think real hard. "Let's see — there's portly, queen size, ample, and stout. And, you know, fat isn't a dirty word, even if some people act like it is. It's just an adjective. And there's always obese, although that's the least favorite of mine." She was trying to lighten the moment for him, to let him know this was a subject that could be discussed.

"Actually, though," she continued. "I really prefer the term full-figured."

"Well, you truly are full-figured," he answered, looking directly at her breasts.

Taken by surprise, all Nella could think to do was slap his arm playfully, and say, "Sam!"

Now it was his turn to laugh at her confusion. "Come on, Jake," he said, taking his son's hand, "let's show Mommy where she can walk."

Nella glanced quickly at Sam, surprised at hearing him refer to her as "Mommy." That was the first time she'd ever heard him use the term. But he didn't seem to realize what he'd said.

He led them down the driveway to the narrow dirt road, and headed south.

"One mile from here is a small bridge across a stream. We call it Milligan's Branch. Obviously, when you get to the bridge and come back, you will have gone two miles. Do you want to walk it now, so you'll know where it is?" he asked.

"Sure!" she responded eagerly.

As they walked, Sam pointed out things that brought back childhood memories. A tree where he had watched his grandfather rob a beehive. A deep ditch that he had wrecked his bike in and broken his arm.

As he talked, Jake ventured ahead of them a few feet. Suddenly Nella became aware of his excited voice saying, "Look, kitty cats!"

Looking to where he was pointing, Nella spotted a female skunk crossing the road, with five baby skunks trailing along behind her. She became aware of the skunks and Jake's intentions at the same time. He was headed straight for the skunks, to try to pet one of them. The mother skunk sensed danger at that moment and stopped in the middle of the road. She unexpectedly stood on her front feet, with her hind feet in the air, over her head, and started swatting the air with her full, bushy tail.

"Jake! Stop!" bellowed Sam.

Half turning toward them, Jake started to argue, " But Daddy — "

"*Robot, halt!*" Nella called in a quiet, yet stern, voice.

Jake stopped dead in his tracks. "*Robot, return to your space commander, now!* Danger is near."

Walking slowly and mimicking a robot, Jake came back to Nella as the family of skunks disappeared into the undergrowth alongside the road.

Nella knelt down and hugged Jake closely. "Robot, you did well in obeying your commander."

"But Mommy, kitty cats aren't dangerwous."

"These aren't regular kitty cats, Son." Sam joined in the conversation, squatting down beside them. "These are in the kitty cat family, but they're wild and live in the woods, and when they get angry or frightened they spray a horrible scent out of their body and it's so bad you have a hard time washing it off."

Just then, as if on cue, a rancid odor surrounded them. Jake wrinkled his nose, and Sam and Nella burst into laughter.

"That, Son, was the mother skunk showing us what she could have done if you had touched one of her babies," Sam explained.

"It *is* horwable," Jake agreed, holding his nose.

"What was she doing standing on her front feet like that?" Nella needed almost as much education on this country living as Jake did.

"She was warning us that she was getting ready to spray us," Sam explained, and then continued, "What was that robot thing you did with Jake?"

"After that creep tried to snatch Jake from me, back in South Carolina, I came up with this game we play. It's fun for Jake, and it keeps him alert. Sometimes just shouting 'no,' or 'come back' doesn't get through to a child, but playing a game will get their attention. I've done it at times when I knew he was involved in something else, just to see if he would respond, and also to teach him to respond. Sometimes he's the space commander, and I'm the robot. We take turns. I've always hoped it would work, and now I know it does. Jake, you were a good robot! I'm proud of you." She hugged him again.

They had almost made it to the one-mile mark when Jake spoke up and said, "My feet are hurting, I guess someone will just have to carry me on their shoulders!"

Sam and Nella laughed, and Sam swung Jake to his shoulders.

They made their way back toward the house and were almost there when Sam suddenly stopped and stood Jake on the ground and knelt beside him. "Son, see this crooked mark in the dirt? See, it goes from one side of the road to the other?"

"Uh-huh," nodded Jake.

"Now, that's where a real snake has been."

Hearing Nella's sharply indrawn breath, he stood and reassured her.

"Oh, it's not a poisonous snake. See, the crooks are wide apart. If the snake is poisonous, the crooks are tight and close together."

"Well, a snake is a snake, as far as I'm concerned," Nella hastened to assure him.

"Don't tell me there's actually something you're afraid of?"

His amusement was so genuine that she decided not to mention spiders at this point.

Chapter 7

A few days later, Nella heard Sam in his office on the phone. She could tell by the tone of his voice and the regular intervals of laughter that he was enjoying the call. He obviously had called the person, as she hadn't heard the phone ring with an incoming call.

Was the party on the other end of the line male or female? She fought the urge to stand by the door and try to hear what Sam was saying, but she did find several reasons to walk past the door and try to hear. It wasn't like her at all, but she'd never heard Sam enjoying himself so much, and it had her curiosity up. Had he called Miranda?

Finally she heard him saying good-bye, and she hurried back to the kitchen to busy herself with some minor chore just in case he came looking for her, which he soon did.

"I was just on the phone with Tommy McCoy. He was my best buddy in high school, and I always call him when I come home. He's one of the best people I know. I really enjoy talking with him. He's real, and down to earth. You always know where you stand with Tommy."

As he talked, Sam made a glass of tea and sat down at the kitchen table. "He married the prettiest girl in our class. Amy Singley. She was the homecoming queen for our class. But even with her looks and popularity, she still had the best personality of anybody around. They make a fantastic couple. You'll love being with them."

"Which sounds like something I'll be doing soon, from that statement." Nella sat down at the table. She was relieved it was an old school friend that Sam had been on the phone with, and not someone from his other world.

"They want us to come see them Friday night. They own a farm not too far down the way from here, and they're having a hayride Friday night. They'll probably roast marshmallows or do something like that. Tommy always has a huge bonfire when he gets a group together like this. They have three children, and I think Jake will really enjoy being there."

"Do they know the nature of your marriage?" Nella asked hesitantly.

"No. I see no reason to go into that. They were very surprised to learn I'd remarried. The last time I talked with them, I was convinced I'd never marry again. But they're wonderfully accepting people. They won't ask any incorrect questions."

The McCoys' home was an older farmhouse with a porch wrapped all the way around it. There were four rocking chairs and two swings on the front section of the porch. It had such a welcoming, homey feel that

Nella felt herself relaxing even before anyone answered the rhythmic knock Sam delivered to the front door.

They heard approaching footsteps, then the door was swung wide by a burly giant of a man with wavy black hair and clear blue eyes. He grabbed Sam in a bear hug, and the two friends embraced like long-lost brothers, laughing and kidding each other at the same time.

Finally Sam turned to Nella and introduced her. She, in turn, was engulfed in a warm, affectionate hug. Then, keeping his hands on her shoulders, the big man held her away from him and looked her up and down.

"Well, Sam, you got yourself a real woman this time. And a beauty, too." He reached down and picked Jake up, and with one arm around Nella's shoulders, said, "Y'all come on in, and let me find Amy. She's in here somewhere. *Amy!*" he bellowed, "Come and see who's here."

A short, plump woman came through the door into the living room. She had the potential of being very pretty, but her long, straight blonde hair was pulled back into a ponytail at the back of her neck, and she didn't have a trace of makeup on. She had startling green eyes that came alive when she saw Sam standing in the room.

"Amy!" he exclaimed warmly, and held his arms open to her. "You're still the prettiest girl in school," he assured her, hugging her tightly.

When she stepped away from him, she gave him a playful slug on the shoulder. "Sam du Cannon, you liar. You know I've gotten fat since I had the children. I may have been the prettiest girl in class, but not anymore."

Nella couldn't believe how she was putting herself down in front of everyone.

"I have to listen to this kind of talk every day," Tommy said. "I keep telling her I love her no matter what size she is, but she just insists she's fat and keeps going on these diets, and I'm afraid she's hurting her health. Sam, you remember Amy's mama and grandma, don't you?" At Sam's confirming nod, the big man continued, "They're both plump women. I knew when I married Amy that she'd probably eventually look just like her mama, but, hell, I always thought her mama was kind of sexy!"

"Tommy!" Amy playfully scolded him, but he continued, "Nella, you try to talk some sense into her, okay?"

Nella smiled at the woman she'd not even been officially introduced to yet.

"Hi, Nella. Don't listen to him. He's always running off at the mouth about something." Amy welcomed Nella with a big hug and a welcoming smile.

Just then, the front door burst open and three children dashed in. They ranged in age from a girl who looked to be about eight to a boy approximately five and another little girl around Jake's age.

"Kids! Slow down. Uncle Sam is here with his wife and son, Jake. Susie," Tommy addressed the oldest girl, "you remember Sam, don't you?"

A young, slim version of Amy answered shyly, "Yes, and his other wife. I didn't like her," she said with a child's honesty.

"Susie!" Amy scolded.

Nella glanced quickly at Jake to see if he realized the girl was talking about his mother, but apparently he hadn't noticed. He was too absorbed in watching the children to actually pay attention to what was being said.

"Sam, why don't you and me take the kids down to the barn and let Jake see the new baby kittens? The girls can get acquainted better without us around. The rest of the gang will be here in a couple of hours and I still have a few things I need to do to get that hay wagon ready."

Sam winked at Nella as if trying to reassure her. He took Jake's hand and followed Tommy through the door.

"Come on," Amy said, turning to leave the living room. "I've got a few more things to do in the kitchen before I change clothes."

Nella offered to help. but Amy insisted that she just sit at the table and drink some tea while Amy "finished up." She informed Nella that they were having a wiener roast before going on the hayride.

"You ever been on a hay ride, Nella?" Amy asked as she washed the last dish and put it in the drain rack.

"No, I haven't, but I've always thought it would be fun," Nella said.

"Oh, you'll love Tommy's hay ride. He'll make sure you have a good time, since this is your first." The green eyes flashed with a mysterious promise of things to come that made Nella slightly nervous.

"What?" she asked.

"Oh, I don't know, myself," Amy hedged, "but I'm sure Tommy will come up with something." She smiled knowingly.

"Well, if you and I are the only ones who know that I've never been on a hay ride, and neither of us tell anyone, then Tommy can't possibly know, can he," Nella reasoned.

"Do you really think he's going to let Sam's new wife get away without being the brunt of his evening's fun? You might as well accept the fact, because it *will* happen," Amy assured her, giggling at the prospect.

Nella felt an immediate liking for Amy, and before long the two women were chatting like they'd known each other for years.

"Well, I guess I need to go change into something different," Amy said after they'd chatted for a while. "I don't know why I even bother, though. One thing I wear looks about as bad as the other." Discouragement sounded in her voice.

"Why do you put yourself down like that?" Nella asked, puzzled.

"I just stay so discouraged all the time about how I look." Amy's answer was genuine.

"Then do something about it," Nella said.

"I've tried! Honestly I have, but the weight just won't come off. And I do try to eat correctly. I cook good, healthy meals for my family, and I don't think I overeat, but in order for me to lose weight I have to cut my calories back so far that I don't have the energy to do my chores and keep up with the children. Then I get bitchy, and that makes everyone unhappy."

"I didn't mean lose weight," Nella interrupted. "You said you were discouraged with how you look. When I said do something about it, I meant fix yourself up, and you'll feel better. Put on some makeup, do your hair differently, wear things that make you feel pretty, and enjoy yourself just the way you are."

"You mean stop trying to lose weight?" The idea seemed foreign to Amy.

"Yes," Nella said. "Tommy said you took after your mother and grandmother. Were they always trying to lose weight?"

"No. In fact, I don't think I ever heard them mention the subject." Amy seemed surprised at the realization.

"Were you embarrassed about their size when you were a child?"

"Heavens, no! That thought never crossed my mind. I always thought my mother was a beautiful lady. She dressed with the best, and always carried herself with pride. I've seen her turn many a head." As Amy talked she realized what she was saying, and the full truth dawned on her. Suddenly her face lit up with hope.

"Nella, I can't believe this. It's taken you, a total stranger, all of one hour to make me realize what Tommy's been saying to me for years. Will you come with me upstairs and help me with my makeover?" Her eyes flashed with excitement.

Amy led Nella upstairs to a large bedroom. The curtains were open, and the room was filled with sunlight. There was a chair by the window, with an open book on the windowsill. Everything in the room looked lived in and comfortable.

Amy sat down at an antique dresser and took the rubber band from her hair. Her hair fell around her face in a full, swinging motion. Nella saw that the natural blond hair that had been restrained by the rubber band was really full and beautiful. Amy started brushing her hair, and it responded with a healthy shine.

"Why would anyone hide hair like that?" Nella asked.

"What?" Amy paused from her brushing and looked at Nella.

"Your hair is beautiful! Why do you pull it back with that rubber band?"

"It's just the easiest way to get it out of my face, I guess," Amy shrugged. She started digging around in the dresser drawers, pulling out miscellaneous containers of makeup. When she had an array placed on top of the dresser she turned to Nella and said, "Okay, tell me which one to use. Your makeup is beautifully done, so you tell me what to do."

Nella looked at the makeup, which was obviously several years old and pretty much outdated, colorwise. "Well, the first thing I would suggest is to go buy some new makeup," she teased. "But in the meantime, I think we can find enough here to use. Did you wear makeup in high school?"

"Sure," Amy confirmed.

"Well, just do what you did then, except we'll change a few things. Don't you have a magazine that you could get some ideas from?"

"Oh, yes! Hold on a minute." Amy dashed from the room, soon returning with a magazine. She pointed at a picture of a pretty blonde with short hair.

"I think she's so pretty. Make me look like her," she exclaimed. She was acting like an excited teenager.

"She has short hair," Nella stated the obvious," but we can try to match the makeup."

"Cut my hair!" Amy suggested.

"What? I can't cut hair," Nella laughed.

"Yes, you can. All you have to do is trim the bottom. See, start here, just below my ear lobe, and cut it all the way around, one length. You'll do fine. That's all they do at the beauty shop when I go."

Nella looked at Amy's hair skeptically. It wouldn't be that hard to cut, and she'd trimmed her friends' hair on a few occasions.

Again Amy jumped up and left the room, returning with a pair of scissors and a towel in her hand. She handed the scissors to Nella and wrapped the towel around her shoulders. "Cut," she instructed.

"What if I mess it up?" Nella asked, a doubtful look on her face.

"Then I'll wear a hat tonight and go have it fixed tomorrow. Just cut."

Amy's mind was made up, so Nella took the scissors and started trimming her hair. Her hand shook a little at first, but she relaxed and did a beautiful job of shortening Amy's existing style. Amy's hair was all the same length and parted on the side. The shorter cut gave her hair even more body, and it bounced each time Amy moved her head.

Nella couldn't believe she was in the bedroom of a woman she had known less than two hours, actually cutting the woman's hair. She was also surprised at how close she felt to Amy. She regretted that she'd probably never see her again after this visit, with her future as unstable as it was. She and Sam could dissolve this farce of a marriage at any time, and Nella would probably never come back to Kentucky. She mentally shook herself back to the present as she finished cutting Amy's hair.

Nella was amazed at the difference the shorter hair made in Amy's appearance. She looked ten years younger. She had a natural, fresh, youthful look, and the shorter hair enhanced it. That gave Nella an idea.

"Amy, I think all you need on your eyes is mascara and a little liner, maybe on the bottom lids, and just a touch of this light green shadow in the corners to enhance the color of your eyes. Then put your foundation on, and use this pink blush, and this light pink lipstick. Put a little loose powder on your eyes before you put the shadow on."

Amy followed Nella's instructions. When she finished, the transformation was breathtaking. She was truly pretty, but she looked more like a teenager than a married woman with three children.

"Oh, Nella," she exclaimed, staring at herself in the mirror, "I haven't looked like this in years, and it feels so good! I can't believe

I've wasted all this time, just waiting until I lost weight to be pretty, when this was all I had to do. How did I allow myself to get so bogged down with my wrong thinking?"

"Amy, nobody's perfect. It doesn't matter who you're talking about. Even the movie stars and beauty queens have flaws they have to work on. They either have them cosmetically fixed or cover them up. We have to work around our bad points, enhance our good points, and be happy with the results. That's a lesson women of all sizes should learn. Now, no more preaching on my part." Nella pretended to be zipping up her mouth.

Amy stood up from the dresser and turned to Nella with tears in her eyes. "Can I hug you?" she asked, with her arms open.

"Sure," Nella said, hugging her tightly.

"Now." Amy broke the embrace and headed for the closet. "What to wear?" She thumbed through the hangers for a few moments before exclaiming, "Yes! Tommy's going to just pass out!" She pulled out a baby blue blouse with long sleeves. There were ruffles on the sleeves and down the front of the blouse. "He bought this for me for my birthday, and I've never worn it. He thinks I don't like it, but I thought it was too pretty to waste on me. But I'll wear it tonight! But with what?" She started back through the closet.

"Jeans," suggested Nella.

"Jeans? A frilly blouse with jeans?"

"Yes, it'll be very sexy," Nella insisted.

"Are you sure?" Doubt was still in Amy's voice.

"Trust me," Nella coaxed. "If you want to knock Tommy's socks off, wear the blouse with jeans."

"Okay, if you say so. But turn around and don't look until I'm dressed. I want you to get the full effect after I'm totally dressed."

Nella turned and looked out the window. She could see the barn at a distance. Sam and Tommy were leaning against the wagon full of hay, and the children were running around laughing and playing. Jake looked like he was having the time of his life. She was glad she was here. She really was enjoying herself.

"Okay, you can look."

Nella turned and gazed in astonishment at the woman in front of her. If she hadn't seen the transition with her own eyes she wouldn't have believed it was the same woman she'd met such a short time ago.

The change wasn't just the outward makeover. There had been a change *inside* Amy. She knew she could be pretty again, and the knowledge was shining through her very being. Her eyes sparkled and her skin glowed with excitement.

"Amy, you look beautiful!" Nella exclaimed.

"I do, don't I? Oh, Nella, how can I ever thank you? But will I wake up tomorrow morning and feel the same way, or will I wake up all discouraged and go back to my old way of feeling?"

"That's your decision. You see what you can be if you want to, but it's your decision whether you spend your days looking your best, or looking your worst. That's a decision we all have to make each day. You're no different than anyone else."

"That's right!" Amy agreed, the previous glimpse of doubt and fear gone.

Nella heard something outside and glanced out the window.

"The men are coming back to the house. You'll get to see their reaction now."

"Oh, Nella, I'm so nervous! What if Tommy doesn't like me like this?"

"Do you like you like this?" Nella asked.

"Of course I do!" Conviction sounded in every word.

"Then that's what matters. But I'm sure Tommy will love this new you. Why don't we go find out? I have an idea! Why don't you stay up here until they get settled in, and then you make a grand entrance. I'll go on down and tell them you're still getting dressed. Give us a few minutes, then come into the room."

"Nella, my teeth are chattering, I'm so nervous." Amy was dancing around like a child.

"I'm gone," Nella said, leaving the room.

She managed to be sitting on the couch with a magazine in her lap when Sam and Tommy entered the living room.

"Well, did my little woman desert you and leave you here all alone to entertain yourself?" Tommy boomed.

"Just for a little while." Nella managed to look natural and hide the excitement she felt.

Sam sat on the couch close beside her and put his arm on the back of the couch behind her shoulders. Having Sam so close gave her a sudden, warm sense of actually belonging to this setting.

"Jake is having a wonderful time," he told her. She could smell the fresh air on him as he leaned close to talk to her.

"He loved the new baby kittens," Tommy added. "I told Sam y'all need to take one home with you for the boy."

"Do you mind?" Sam asked, almost looking like a kid himself.

"Of course, I don't mind, but what will we do when we travel?" Reality struck home on Sam's face, and he looked disappointed.

"Yeah, I forgot about that," he murmured.

He forgot? Sam du Cannon forgot that he traveled? This fresh air must have really gotten to his brain.

Just then Nella heard Amy's footsteps coming down the hallway, and she prepared herself for what was about to happen. But nothing could have prepared her for Tommy's reaction when Amy entered the room.

Amy's uncertainty was in evidence, causing her to look shy and bashful, which only added to and enhanced her youthful look.

"What the hell?" Tommy was on his feet, now looking at his wife as if a stranger had entered the room. Nella heard a surprised, indrawn breath from Sam.

"Do you like me like this? Please say you do," Amy pleaded quietly.

"Like you?" Tommy's voice was hushed, as if he could barely get it out. He was like an awestruck teenager. "Baby, welcome back. I've missed this you so much!" And he went to her and gathered her close in his arms. Soon he let her go, just enough to hold her at arms length and look at her again. His eyes were blurred with tears and he rubbed at them to clear his vision. "You look beautiful! Look at her, Sam. She looks just like she did the night she was Homecoming Queen."

Amy was relaxing, now, knowing her new look had been accepted.

"You do look beautiful, Amy," Sam agreed. "I'm very impressed." And he was. It had been a long time since he'd seen Amy look like she cared about herself at all. In fact, there had been times when he'd wondered if she were happy with her marriage and life.

"What brought all this on? And who cut your hair?" Tommy asked.

Amy pointed at Nella.

"Ah, yes, I should have known," Sam said quietly, for Nella's ears only.

"Nella convinced me that I didn't need to keep putting my life off until I lost weight. In fact, Tommy, she told me the same thing you've always said about me taking after Mama and Grandmere, but it just finally sunk in when another person said it. I'm sorry I've wasted all this time looking my worst and making you look at me. I promise from now on, I'm going to take more pride in myself. In fact," her excitement was bubbling over, now that she knew her husband liked her new look, "tomorrow, I'm going shopping! I have a great idea. Sam, Nella, why don't you spend the night so Nella can go shopping with me and help me look for some things? It'll be late tonight when the hay ride is over anyway, and you don't need to drive home late at night."

Nella was about to say why that plan wouldn't work when Sam answered, "That sounds like a great idea to me. Sure, we'll stay."

Nella looked at him as if he had taken leave of his senses, but he just grinned at her and winked.

Suddenly the children stormed through the front door. Jake came directly to Sam and Nella, but the other three children stopped abruptly and stared open-mouthed at their mother.

"Mom?" Susie asked.

"Mama, you look beautiful," their son, Daniel, exclaimed, as if this were something he didn't think was possible.

"Mom!" Susie repeated. "You look like a movie star!"

They all laughed at her declaration.

A car horn blaring in the driveway announced someone's arrival. It was the first of many more vehicles.

Nella was amazed at the scene taking place around her. People were arriving with food and extra chairs. Before long the large front porch was covered with people. A huge bonfire was burning in the yard and children ran and played everywhere. Nella worried about Jake briefly, but Sam assured her Susie would keep an eye out for him. She checked on him occasionally, and sure enough, Susie was always close to him.

Nella listened to the flow of conversation around her. These people were proud of their heritage. They were proud of their state of Kentucky and of the part it played in the early settling of the country. She heard conversations about Daniel Boone and how he blazed the trail through the Cumberland Gap and tried to establish Kentucky as the fourteenth American colony. In fact, several people wore coonskin caps.

A small group had gathered with guitars, a banjo, and a fiddle, and was playing bluegrass music. Nella liked the music okay, but the songs seemed sad, and she couldn't listen to it long without feeling depressed. She knew, though, that some people thought the music had a happy sound.

What amazed her most was how well Sam fit in with this group. He seemed as relaxed, and maybe more so, with these rural people as he did with his business peers at the company party in Hawaii. As she watched him he looked up and caught her eyes on him. He smiled and winked at her and continued conversing with the guys gathered around him.

"It's good to see Sam happy." Amy had come up beside Nella, and had seen the look that had just passed between them. "It's so obvious he's happy with you, and I'm sorry, but he just never seemed happy with Vanessa. She was a hard woman to like. I never could figure out why Sam married her."

Nella was speculating on an answer, but none was needed as Amy continued. "Nella, I can't remember when I've had so many compliments! Thanks again. I'll always love you for helping me come to my senses today."

"Can I have everyone's attention, please?" Tommy was trying to talk over the hubbub of the crowd. Slowly everyone quieted down and listened to him.

"We've got a table over here with all the hotdog fixin's. We've got sticks cut that you can use to roast your wieners, so come on, let's feed our faces, then we'll have some real fun on the hay ride."

"Do you know how to do this?" Sam was at her side with three sticks in his hand.

"No, I'm afraid I don't," she said, looking skeptically at the sticks he was holding. Someone had apparently just cut some twigs off of trees for this purpose.

Susie came up with Jake, and Sam took his hand and told Nella to follow him. He led them to the table, where they got three wieners. He showed Nella and Jake how to put a wiener on a stick, and they found an empty spot beside the bonfire. He showed her how to hold her wiener in the fire so it would cook, turning it slowly so it didn't burn in one place. Then he helped Jake hold and turn his.

Nella was amazed at how good the hotdogs tasted, cooked this way.

Tommy and Amy came over and sat with Sam and Nella while they ate their meal. Nella was amused at Tommy's attentiveness to Amy. He was openly flirting with his wife, and she was enjoying every moment of it.

Chapter 8

"Okay, everyone," Tommy called above the voices, "everybody who wants to go on this hay ride, mount up!"

He indicated two wagons of hay behind him. Nella had wondered how all these people could possibly get on one wagon, but Tommy had connected two wagons, each stacked with baled hay. At least it was baled and not loose, making it easier to sit on without sliding off. To Nella's astonishment a pair of horses was hooked to the wagons, not a tractor, as she had expected.

"Horses?" she asked Sam, who was standing beside her with Jake, who was anxious to get on the hay.

"Yeah, this is a real hay ride," Sam said roguishly.

"Could I have everyone's attention, please?" Tommy was again trying to talk. People stopped climbing up onto the hay to hear what he wanted to say.

"I think since Nella is our newest addition to the group — "
Suddenly Nella remembered Amy's warnings. " — that she should
drive the horses."

"Yeah!" Everyone cheered the suggestion.

Nella waited patiently until the cheering had quieted down before
saying, "Oh, I don't really think so." Determination sounded in every
word.

"But you have to," Tommy insisted, and the group cheered again,
agreeing with him.

Nella couldn't help but believe it was a set-up. "Look, people, I
know nothing about hay rides, and even less about horses. Trust me,
you don't want your lives in my hands."

Sam placed his arm around Nella's shoulders and whispered, "The
horses know the route we'll be taking. They've done this enough to
do it if no one was guiding them. All you have to do is hold the reins,
and they'll do the rest."

The only thing Nella knew about horses was what she had seen
on the western movies she used to watch with her father, and she
was sure that didn't qualify her to actually deal with live horses,
especially when so many people were involved. She knew horses were
fairly easy to spook. What if something frightened one of them and
they ran away like in the movies? The thought caused her to shake
her head.

"No, Sam, I — " But he stopped her with a finger on her lips.

"Come on, be a good sport," he whispered. "Tommy's having a
blast with this. He doesn't believe you'll do it, and he's enjoying
making you squirm. Show him what spunk you have. I'll stay close to
you in case something happens, which it won't."

Nella looked deep into Sam's eyes. For some reason he really wanted her to do this, although she couldn't for the life of her understand why. But if it meant that much to Sam, she' surely give it a try.

"Well, what are we waiting for?" Nella asked the eagerly awaiting group. "Let's go!" And she climbed up into the wagon's seat.

"Well, I'll be damned!" Tommy swore. "I didn't think she'd do it. No one else has ever taken my baiting seriously before."

"I dare say you've never met anyone like Nella before, friend," Sam assured him. "You go sit back there by your wife. I'll sit here and help guide these mules."

"Mules, hell, you know this is the finest pair of working horses in this county," Tommy bragged as he plopped down beside Amy.

The hay had been arranged on one of the wagons to form a deep square section for the smaller children to sit in so they wouldn't fall off. Everyone else perched wherever they could find a spot.

Sam took the reins in his hands and reached around Nella's shoulders with one arm. Then, placing the reins in her hands, he showed her how to hold them to guide the horses. "See — " he was so close his breath fanned her hair. "If you want to go right, you gently pull the rein in your right hand. To go left, you pull to the left. You don't have to pull hard, just tug enough so the horses know what you want from them. Now, if you're just letting them walk straight, you just hold the reins loosely like this, and if you want to stop, you pull back just enough for them to feel the bit in their mouths, and they'll respond."

Sam turned the reins over to her, but didn't move away. She didn't mind, though, because she'd quickly hand him the reins if anything went wrong, and the closer he was, the better. Although his thigh pressing against hers was more distracting than she wanted to admit.

Once the horses were in motion down the old road and they had gotten away from the lights of the house, Nella realized that the moon was full and bright. They really didn't need any kind of light to see where they were going. The night was beautiful. The light breeze that fanned her hair was cool, but not enough to chill, and the sky was so clear it seemed as if she could see a million stars. Nella breathed in the fresh, sweet smell of the hay, and the pleasant night scents that surrounded them.

The people on the hay behind them were laughing and telling stories. Someone had brought along a harmonica and was playing a happy melody.

"How often do they do this?" Nella asked, turning to Sam.

"Usually someone in the community has a gathering about once a month. It helps keep everyone in the community close to each other." He held her gaze with his. The moonlight caught and glinted off his eyes.

"Okay, you two newlyweds don't get mushy up there and spook the horses," someone yelled.

Sam smiled. "You know, they do expect us to show some kind of affection for each other. They're all back there being romantic in this beautiful moonlight, and they've all been married longer than we have. I think I might need to kiss you. Just for their sake, of course." The smile on his face was teasing. He was deliberately trying to intimidate her.

"I think maybe you should," she said, determined not to be outdone, but not really believing he'd kiss her.

But Sam, accepting the challenge, lifted his hand from the back of the wagon seat and buried it in her thick, luxurious hair. He tilted her head slightly back and toward him, and slowly lowered his lips to hers.

Caught off guard, Nella's hand holding the reins gave a quick, jerking motion, causing the horses to come to an abrupt stop.

Several people almost fell off the hay because of the sudden stop, and began yelling, "What's going on?" When they discovered Sam and Nella they all started whistling and giving wolf calls.

"Atta boy, Sam," someone yelled.

Slowly releasing Nella, Sam cleared his throat and took the reins from her. He quietly clucked to the horses. They started back in motion, instantly. Someone started singing an old song, and everyone joined in.

"What happened back there?" Nella asked.

"I kissed you." Sam's voice was teasing again.

"No, not that!" Nella scolded. "Why did the horses stop so suddenly?"

"You apparently jerked back on the reins, and to a horse that means stop, remember?" Sam reminded her of the lesson he had given earlier.

"Oh." She knew that. She just didn't realize she'd jerked the reins when Sam kissed her.

Sam handed the reins back to her, but Nella pushed his hand away. "That's okay, you can do it now. No telling what I might make those horses do next."

But Sam took her hand and placed the reins in it.

"When I decide to kiss you again, I'll warn you not to make any sudden moves."

Nella knew Sam was teasing her, but her already racing pulse quickened even more, especially since he had said "when," not "if," he decided to kiss her again.

The horses plodded along at a slow, steady pace. Some of the people in back of them were singing, some were talking, and some just sat enjoying the night, the company, and the moonlight.

In a little while, Tommy said, "Okay, Sam, you know what the spot ahead is, and you know what the tradition is. You do remember, don't you?"

"I remember, Tommy," Sam assured his friend, and as the wagons drew close to a huge boulder beside the road, he reached over and took the reins from Nella. As they got even with the boulder, Sam stopped the horses.

"See the formation at the top of the boulder? It looks like two people kissing. This has become known as Kissing Boulder, and it has been the tradition of lovers down through the years to always stop here and kiss when they pass by. It's supposed to bring them good luck. It's also the tradition of all of Tommy's hayrides to stop the hay wagons and all the lovers on the ride kiss each other. And I think all of our friends back there are waiting for us to set the example." Sam placed a hand on each side of Nella's face and lowered his lips to hers. The kiss was long and probing and gentle, causing Nella's entire body to dissolve into limp pulp.

"Sam, Nella, look at this," Tommy called.

Jake and the McCoys' youngest daughter, Sarah, were locked in an embrace and busy kissing. They stopped when everyone started laughing at them.

"Hey, maybe we'll be in-laws some day," Amy suggested.

Sam started the horses, but this time he held onto the reins.

Nella's heart was pounding in her chest, and she felt as if she might hyperventilate, she was breathing so hard. Sam's kiss had been very passionate and real. The cool air burned her hot, flushed skin. She had to calm down before Sam noticed.

As Sam watched the moonlight play off the horses' backs, he wondered what had possessed him to kiss Nella like he had. He could still feel her soft lips yielding to his, and he felt a hunger to taste more. This moonlight was having a strange effect on him tonight, for sure.

The horses rounded another curve and the McCoy farmhouse lay before them.

"How did we do that, without making any turns?" Nella asked, thoroughly puzzled, as Sam stopped the horses in front of the house.

Sam laughed. "Tommy has a utility road that circles his farm. That way, he can check his fencerows as he drives, and he doesn't have to walk them out. It's the lazy man's way."

"It's the smart man's way," interjected Tommy, who had just come up behind them.

Soon everyone said good night, and left for home.

"Come on in and let's have some coffee and talk some more. It's still early." Tommy had his arm around Amy's shoulders.

"We'll make the kids a pallet in the living room and let Jake sleep with them if it's okay. That'll give you the whole room to yourselves." Amy was busy making sleeping arrangements.

"Sure," Sam agreed, again before Nella could come up with a reason to protest. "Jake is having such a good time with your children."

And Jake really *was* having a wonderful time. Nella had hardly seen him since they'd arrived here. To her surprise, she actually missed having him underfoot all the time.

After the kids were settled on the living room floor "camping out," as they were pretending to do, the two couples gathered around the dining room table with their cups of coffee.

Nella listened to the three friends reminisce about their high school days. They laughed at stories they remembered. Sam asked about people in the area he hadn't heard from in years. Nella was amazed at the insight she gained about Sam just from listening to them talk.

They talked for hours. Finally Tommy looked at the clock and yawned and stretched. "People, it's one thirty. If we plan to get up in the morning, we'd better go to bed."

Nella had been dreading this moment all night. How would Sam handle the situation? How would she handle it? She'd soon find out. Maybe there'd be twin beds in the room.

The children had long been asleep, and the house was quiet.

"Sam, you know where the guest room is. You slept there before when you and — " Tommy stopped, knowing he had talked himself into a corner. Embarrassment washed over his face.

"It's okay, Tommy," Nella assured him. "I do know Sam was married before. Don't worry about it."

"Thanks for understanding my big mouth," he murmured.

They all said good night, and Nella followed Sam to a closed door across from the living room. He walked into the room and switched on the light.

The room was large, like the bedroom upstairs, but this one contained a bedroom suite with a king-size bed.

Nella was disappointed that they didn't find twin beds in the room, but a king-size was better than a regular full-size bed would have been.

"Pretty impressive for a guest room," Nella observed, trying to keep the relief from her voice. At least they wouldn't have to spend the night trying to avoid touching each other.

"Tommy and Amy bought this for themselves, then didn't like it because it was too big, so they went back to a queen-size and put this one in here," Sam explained.

There were two rocking chairs in the room. The decor was country, and the bed was covered in a beautiful, hand-stitched quilt. The room was relaxing and comforting, but Nella didn't feel relaxed or comfortable. She was about to spend the night in the same bed with Sam, and she had nothing to sleep in.

This was not a good situation. She could ask Amy for something, but that would look odd, since most married couples wouldn't mind sleeping nude with their mate, at least occasionally.

"I can't believe you let us get into this situation, Sam!" Nella said, turning on him.

"It's okay, Nella. It's a big bed. Trust me, you won't even know I'm there. Now I'll just jump in the bathroom first, then you can take as long as you like." He went directly to the adjoining bathroom, where Nella could hear him stirring around.

Suddenly she felt irritation at Sam for allowing them to be in this situation, and for being so nonchalant about it. It stood to reason, though, if he weren't attracted to her that it wouldn't bother him to sleep in the same bed with her, even if she were naked. Maybe she would put him to the test. She ought to just strip down and be waiting under the covers for him and see if he would even notice. He—

"Amy usually keeps extra sleeping apparel in some of those drawers for unexpected overnight guests, if you want to check it out," Sam said, sticking his head around the door from the bathroom, a toothbrush in his mouth. "Oh, and there are toothbrushes in here if you want one. Unused, of course." He grinned around the toothbrush that hung precariously from his mouth.

Relief flooded Nella as she went to the chest of drawers to look for something to sleep in. The McCoys sure knew how to make a person feel welcome in their home.

She pulled out a drawer that contained women's nightgowns and pajamas. The items weren't new, but they were clean and smelled fresh. She found a pink nightgown she thought would fit her fairly well.

Finally Sam came from the bathroom. "Your turn," he said, and sat on the bed and started taking off his shoes.

Nella was impressed with the bathroom. Everything a person could need was in easy reach. The thought of a shower suddenly seemed inviting to her. Maybe if she took time to shower, Sam would have the light off and be asleep when she went back to the bedroom.

She finished her shower and dried off. She slipped into the gown she had chosen, and was dismayed to find that it fit everywhere except her breasts. The bodice barely covered half her breasts, and even worse, the snug fit had a "push up" effect. Oh, well, some women went to parties with clothes on that fit like this. Surely she could sleep in the gown for one night in a dark room.

She turned the bathroom light off and quietly opened the door a little to peek into the bedroom. Thank goodness, the light was out, so Sam must be in bed, and hopefully asleep.

As her eyes adjusted to the darkness, she realized Sam had opened the bedroom curtains, and moonlight flooded the room. Under more normal circumstances, she would have reveled in the moonlight, but tonight she would rather have done without it.

She hung her clothes across the back of one of the chairs and was about to go across the room to the bed when a movement outside the window caught her eye. She went closer to the window to look out, and there, just a few yards from her, was a female doe with two fawns that still had their spots.

Nella forgot Sam and the moonlight, and everything except the beautiful sight outside the window. She eased down on the window seat, trying not to startle the animals with any sudden movement. Soon two more deer came out of the woods and approached the house, slowly making their way to join the others. Apparently they were grazing on the grass of the lawn.

"Now that's a beautiful picture." Sam's voice invaded the quiet room.

Startled, Nella looked in the direction of his voice. He wasn't in bed at all, but in a rocking chair beside the bed. Apparently he had been sitting there looking out the window all the time. He pulled the chair closer, into the full moonlight, and Nella could tell he only had on his jeans. He had pulled off his shirt, shoes and socks, and was sitting and enjoying the sight outside the window when she had come from the bathroom.

"Yes, it's a beautiful sight," Nella agreed, turning back to look out the window, but wanting desperately to run for cover.

Sam didn't tell her that he wasn't just referring to the animals outside, but to her, as she sat in the full moonlight watching the grazing animals. The scene looked like some classic Victorian oil painting.

Suddenly one of the deer raised its head and snorted, and they all bounded quickly into the woods.

"Well, I guess nature's show is over for now," Nella said, rising from the window seat. She was relieved to be able to escape the moonlight. She was about to go to the far side of the bed when Sam got up and walked around to the same side and started unbuckling his belt.

Choosing not to argue the point, Nella took the side of the bed closest to the window. As she quickly got under the sheet, she realized that her side of the bed was flooded with moonlight. Throwing the sheet aside and starting to get up, she said, "I'm going to close the curtains.'

"No," Sam's voice stopped her. "I like the view."

"Then you sleep on this side of the bed," she told him.

"No. I like the view from this side of the bed," he persisted.

"That doesn't make sense," Nella said in exasperation, plopping back down on her back, forgetting temporarily about her sheet.

"Oh, if you could see my view from here, you wouldn't say that." Nella heard the teasing note in his voice, and looking down saw the top part of her body bathed in the soft light. She quickly grabbed the sheet and pulled it close around her neck, turning her back to Sam.

She heard his soft chuckle as he settled into bed.

Weary from her day, Nella was sure she would soon fall fast asleep. But as she closed her eyes tightly to shut out the bright moonlight, the memory of Sam sitting in the rocking chair, watching the deer, popped into her mind's eye. He had made a striking picture sitting there. The moonlight had been bright enough to let Nella get a full view of his broad shoulders and chest. She could remember exactly how the light reflected across the hair on his chest.

Sleep eluded her. After a while, starting to feel uncomfortable, she wanted to turn over but didn't know how close Sam was to her, or if he were facing her. She sure didn't want him to know she was still awake. It was going to be a long night. She lay for a long, miserable time before finally falling asleep.

Sam, too, lay awake for a long time, remembering the day with his friends. He realized he'd missed being around good, honest people. Not that the people he worked with weren't honest, but the concept of life was just so different here.

He thought of the change Nella had helped bring to Amy. The woman beside him kept surprising him. Most people never surprised him, but Nella seemed to be a constant source of surprises. As he lay thinking about her she moaned softly and turned onto her back. The motion of turning had worked the sheet back to her waist, and again he had a full view of her breasts lighted by the moonlight. His first impulse was to reach out and touch them. They seemed so firm and full.

"Damn!" he muttered, turning his back to her. He should have let her have the dark side of the bed.

The house was quiet when Nella came awake. She could see sunlight outside the window, but everybody still seemed to be asleep. The only sound around was a rooster crowing somewhere in the distance. Maybe that was what had woke her up.

She lay facing Sam, who was on his back with one arm behind his head and the other hand resting on his stomach. The sheet had worked its way down below his waist. The dark hair that covered his chest worked its way to a point just as it entered his white jockey shorts. The hair on his lower arms was dark and curly, and just a sprinkling of the dark curls covered the tops of his well-groomed hands and fingers. Everything about the man, she decided, reeked with sexual energy.

As she watched, he suddenly mumbled something and turned and threw his arm across her, just below her breasts. Subconsciously realizing that he was touching a woman's soft body, he smiled in his sleep and moved his hand up to cup one of her breasts. She tried to move away, but he held her more tightly, and in so doing, his hand pulled the bodice of her gown down to allow her breast to slip free of its protection. Just as she reached to push Sam's hand away, a sharp knock sounded on the door.

"Breakfast is almost ready, sleepyheads," Tommy called. "Up and at 'em."

Nella froze at the loud knock on the door, her hand on Sam's, and that's what Sam saw when his eyes popped open. His hand on her naked breast, with her hand covering his.

"And I thought I was dreaming," he grinned sheepishly.

Nella jumped from bed and headed for the bathroom to dress. Glancing in the vanity mirror, she was mortified to see how flushed her face was from the encounter. She kept patting cold water on her cheeks as she dressed and combed her hair, trying to get her face back to a more normal color.

Sam was still smiling when Nella came from the bathroom.

"You know, Tommy and Amy might want us to spend another few nights with them. What do you think?" He seemed to be reveling in her agitated state.

"What I think," she assured him pointedly, "is that we will not be spending one more night here."

He was softly chuckling as she left the room.

Nella went to the kitchen in search of Amy, whom she found preparing a large breakfast of biscuits, bacon, eggs and oatmeal.

"We don't always eat this kind of breakfast," she explained, "only on special occasions." She had already dressed in slacks and a pink shirt, and her face was made up exactly like the day before. Her eyes glowed with happiness.

"Where are the kids?" Nella asked. She wanted to see Jake.

"They're on the porch with the kittens."

Nella went to the front door to find all four children sitting on the floor of the porch, each holding a kitten. When Jake saw Nella come through the door, he held up a little black and white kitten. "This one's mine, Mommy. Uncle Tommy said I could have it."

"Honey, I don't think — "

"I think we should let him keep it, at least for now." Sam's voice was close behind her.

"But, Sam, it's cruel to let him have a kitten, but later have to leave it if we can't take it with us."

"We'll work something out. I just don't want him to be disappointed."

"Well, it's your decision." Nella gave in with a shrug of her shoulders.

"Not any more. It's our decision, now. And if you don't think it's a good thing to let him have a pet, then I'll tell him, but I don't think it'll cause a problem we can't handle."

"Okay," Nella agreed, still surprised when Sam insisted she be a part of the decision-making when it came to Jake's happiness.

"Son," Sam knelt beside Jake and stroked the kitten. "We're going to let you bring the kitten home, but there might be times when we travel that we'll have to leave it at a place that baby-sits animals, until we get back home. Do you understand that?"

"Yes," Jake quickly agreed, holding the kitten close. "And I've named him Skunk," the child announced proudly. "Because he looks like the skunks we saw on the road."

After the breakfast dishes were finished, Nella and Amy went into Bowling Green to shop for Amy's new look. The first stop they made was a department store, where Amy got a facial with all the tips on how to apply makeup and how to choose the colors that were correct for her. Then they shopped for a few items of clothing. She was like a child at Christmas.

They returned to the McCoy farm during the middle of the afternoon, and Sam, Nella, and Jake said their good-byes and "headed back up the hill," as Sam referred to the mountain they had to climb to get back to his place.

Jake was totally involved with his new pet. He talked to it constantly, and insisted that Skunk sleep with him when it came time to go to bed. Sam and Nella reluctantly gave in, knowing it was a bad habit to start, but Jake looked so contented lying in bed with his hand on the kitten.

Chapter 9

Nella came slowly awake. Her room was dark, so she knew it was still night. The lighted dial on her clock told her it was three a.m. She became aware of two things at once: the howling sound the wind was making outside her window, and the fact that she was very cold.

Two weeks had passed since they'd been to the McCoys'. It was November, and Sam had mentioned just yesterday that it could turn cold anytime. Well, it seemed he was correct, because Nella was cold, and she needed more cover.

She reluctantly got out of the bed, feeling the chill air in the room go right through her thin nightgown. She was sure Jake would be cold and need more cover also.

As her feet touched the cold hardwood floor another blast of wind hit the house and made a low moaning sound. Nella slipped her robe on and went to the window to look out. She was amazed to see snowflakes flying everywhere. The ground was beginning to turn white. Surely this couldn't be happening in November? It wasn't even Thanksgiving yet!

She went to the hall closet and took out a couple of quilts Sam had said his grandmother had made. She took one into Jake's room and spread it on him. He stirred momentarily, then continued to sleep. Skunk lay curled at the foot of the bed. Nella made sure the kitten was on top of the covers, then leaned down and kissed Jake's cheek.

As she stood and turned to leave the room she saw Sam standing in the doorway. The dim glow from the nightlight in Jake's room barely outlined Sam's large frame. She tiptoed toward him, and saw he had a quilt in his hands.

"I guess we had the same idea," he whispered as she came through the door.

"Did the cold wake you up?" she asked.

"Yes. I was shocked at how cold it is in the house. I guess I need to turn on the radio or television and try to hear the weather occasionally. I've basically left the outside world outside since I've been here."

"Speaking of outside, have you looked out the window?" Nella asked.

"No, why?"

"Follow me," she instructed, leading him to the sliding glass doors in the living room, where she pulled back the drapes.

The snow seemed to be swirling even harder and faster now than when she'd looked out the first time.

"I can't believe this!" Sam exclaimed in surprise. "It doesn't usually snow this early in the fall. It's usually more in January and

February when we get snow. Surely this is just going to be a light shower. It'll probably stop soon, and will all be gone by morning. I want Jake to see it in the morning. We'll try to wake him up before the sun comes up and melts it."

Sam noticed Nella shiver and wrap her arms closer around herself, so he draped the quilt around her shoulders to help ward off the cold air.

"Thanks," she said, but never took her eyes off the scene before her. "It's beautiful." She continued watching the falling snow as it swirled and blew. She'd only seen snow a few times in her childhood, and she was still in awe of it.

Sam stood beside her, but he was looking at her instead of the snow. "You like it?" he asked, seemingly surprised.

"Oh! I love it!" she said, excitement threading her voice.

"Vanessa and I spent Christmas here the first year we were married, and it snowed. We were snowed in for a week, and couldn't get back to 'civilization,' as she called it, in time for all the New Year's parties. She bitched every day until the snow thawed. I always loved snow until that year. She made me hate it, and I haven't been back to see a good winter storm since. I didn't realize until just now how much I've missed it."

He stepped closer to Nella and draped an arm around her shoulder.

"When I was a child, if I woke up during the night like this and it was snowing, I'd get dressed and go outside and stand in it, or sit in the porch swing and watch it. I knew I wouldn't have to go to school the next day, so I'd be doubly excited."

"Can we go outside now?" Nella asked.

119

"Sure! Go get some shoes on. We won't stay long. That wind's blowing pretty hard."

Nella went to her room and slipped on a pair of house slippers. She knew they wouldn't keep her feet warm long. She kept the quilt wrapped around her shoulders. That should be enough if they weren't going to stay out very long.

Sam was waiting for her at the door. He'd slipped on some jeans and a black leather jacket.

They went outside and sat in the porch swing. She was surprised when he sat so close to her their bodies touched, and placed his arm on the back of the swing behind her shoulders.

She breathed in deeply and felt the cold air fill her lungs. "Oh, just smell it!" she exclaimed. "This is beautiful. Oh, Sam, I just love this." She was as excited as a child. Just then a strong blast of wind whipped around them, and Nella giggled and pulled the quilt closer.

Sam put his arm around her shoulder and pulled her closer to him. "Cold?" he asked, close to her ear.

"Maybe just excited," she said, looking up at him. Acting on sheer impulse and the excitement of the moment, Nella reached up and kissed Sam on the lips.

For her it was an innocent, spontaneous act, but suddenly she found herself wrapped in Sam's arms as he was kissing her hungrily.

Completely forgetting the quilt, she lifted her free hand to the back of Sam's head to pull him closer. His hand slid inside the quilt, then inside her robe, to come in contact with the flimsy material of her nightgown. He gently massaged a breast as their kiss deepened. His thumb massaged her nipple through the lace of her gown, causing it to harden in response to his touch. His lips left her mouth and traveled down her cheek and neck and were about to join his thumb when suddenly the porch light was flashed on to reveal Jake standing inside the sliding glass doors, holding his kitten and shouting, "Mommy! Daddy! What are you doing outside? And why is the rain white?"

Gathering the quilt quickly around Nella, Sam stood up and, keeping his arm around her shoulders, brought her to a standing position with him. Together they went inside to find Jake in his pajamas, shaking from cold.

Sam picked him up and turned back to the snow outside. "That's snow, Son, not rain. Now if you'll go back to bed and sleep the rest of the night, we'll play in the snow tomorrow, and I'll show you how to make a snowman."

"I'm cold in my bed. Can I sleep with Mommy?" Jake asked his father.

"Seems like we're having the same thoughts tonight, Son," Sam told Jake, while looking at Nella intently.

"Huh?" The child was lost as to what his father meant.

"You need to ask Nella if you can sleep with her. I'm not the one to make that decision."

"Yes, Jake, you can sleep with me tonight," Nella said, although she doubted she'd do much sleeping.

Sam carried Jake to Nella's bed and tucked him in. Then he took the quilt from Nella's shoulders and spread it on the bed. He touched her cheek gently with the tips of his fingers before letting them trail down her cheek, and on down to encircle her neck. Then, bending down, he kissed her lightly on the lips.

"Good night," he whispered.

The shiver that passed over her was not from the cold. Nella slid under the covers, knowing there would be no more sleep for her tonight. Jake snuggled close to her, and was soon warm and fast asleep.

But as she had expected, sleep eluded her. What was happening with Sam? He was so different here in the country. Especially since they'd spent the night at the McCoys' house. He was like a different person. And why had he kissed her so passionately tonight? Maybe if she'd controlled her own impulse and not kissed him, he wouldn't have acted like he did. How far would it have gone if Jake hadn't flashed the light on them?

Did Sam just need a woman because he'd been so long without one? He'd said he wouldn't be attracted to her. Was that changing? Was he beginning to actually care for her?

No. She knew that would never happen.

Was she beginning to care for him?

Damn! Where did that come from?

Suddenly her mindless wandering came to complete attention. Was she beginning to care for Sam du Cannon? He was, she would be the first to admit, one of the most virile, potent, masculine, and yes, handsome men she had ever known. And, she admitted, she was very affected by him, but any normal woman would react the same way to a man like Sam.

Yes, that was it. She was just a normal, red-blooded American woman. She had to convince herself that was the only reason she went weak all over when he kissed her. She had entered this agreement with the security that all she had to do was love Jake. There was no way she could love a jerk like Sam du Cannon.

"But he's not really a jerk, down deep," a little voice inside her head whispered as she drifted off to sleep.

Nella's sleep-muddled mind awoke to the smell of fresh-brewed coffee. She slowly opened her eyes to find Sam standing beside her bed with two cups in his hands.

"Wake up, Sleeping Beauty, we've got a snowman to build, and snowball fights to have."

She smiled lazily and sat up in bed, propping the pillows behind her to give her some support. The covers fell to her waist as she reached for the cup of coffee Sam handed to her. She looked up to find him gazing at the unexpected view being offered to him.

With her free hand, Nella pulled the sheet up under her arms to cover herself. When Sam looked up and met her eyes, there was a soft glow in his.

"I'm sorry," he said sheepishly, sitting on the side of the bed. "I find I'm becoming intrigued with some of your assets."

"Thanks for the coffee." Nella tried to change the subject. This conversation was coming too soon after her thoughts of the night before.

"I went down and lit the furnace this morning, and built a fire in the fireplace, so the house is beginning to warm up now. It snowed about three inches, and Jake is driving me crazy to get out and play in it, but he doesn't have any warm clothes."

"Neither do I, since we came here directly from Hawaii. In fact, where did you get that jacket you had on last night?"

"Oh, that was one of my old jackets that I leave here. Actually, I hadn't given warm clothes any thought, since I'd only planned to stay up here a couple of weeks. But I've enjoyed it so much I haven't wanted to leave."

"What about your work? Don't you miss it?"

"My work goes on whether I'm there or not. I hire the most competent people I can find so things are done the way I want them done, even in my absence. Of course, I keep in touch with them by phone, so I know all is well."

"But don't you miss the hands-on work, and being in the middle of what's happening?"

"This time last year, I would have, but now I don't. Since I've had Jake around so much, I think my values are changing. I don't understand it myself, but I really don't miss my work. I don't know if this is just a passing state of mind that I'm going through, or if it's permanent, but, no, I don't miss it at all."

"So how are we going to play in the snow without warm clothes?" Nella asked.

"I guess I'll have to go down to Bowling Green and buy you and Jake a few items to get by on until we can all go on a shopping spree. The snow won't melt today. The temperature isn't supposed to get over freezing all day. I listened to the weather earlier. We're having unseasonably cold weather for this time of year. But occasionally, we do have these cold snaps."

"Will it be safe to drive in this snow?" Concern sounded in her voice.

"There's only a few inches, and I don't believe it's going to get any worse, and of course, it'll be safe! Remember, I grew up driving these hills under these conditions. I'm an old pro."

From out of nowhere, a sobering thought struck Nella.

"Sam, what would we do if we got snowbound up here?" Her eyes grew large just at the thought.

She had forgotten to hold the sheet as they talked, and it had gradually worked its way back down almost to her waist.

"Right now, that doesn't sound like a bad situation to be in at all." Sam's voice was soft and husky as his eyes took in the soft, alluring skin that showed from the top of her nightgown. Nella quickly pulled the sheet back up.

Chuckling softly, Sam stood up.

"When you get dressed, I'll show you something that should put your mind at ease about getting snowbound, as remote a possibility as that is. I'll go check on Jake."

Wondering what was in store for her now, Nella hurriedly dressed in the warmest clothes she could find and went to the kitchen, where she heard Jake talking. He was just finishing a bowl of cereal.

"Mommy, Mommy," he started as soon as he saw her. "Daddy's going to town to get me some warm clothes so I can play in the snow!" His excitement overflowed with each word.

"I know, sweetheart, won't that be fun?" she said, leaning over and kissing his cheek.

"Are you finished, Jake?" Sam had come over to stand beside them.

At Jake's nod, Sam reached down and lifted him from the chair. Then, taking Nella's hand, he led them to the door to the basement steps. He let go of Nella's hand to unlock the door with a key that hung on a nail beside the door. After putting the key back, he opened the door and flipped on a light switch.

The usual dank, moist basement odor greeted them as they descended the stairs. When they reached the bottom step, Sam made a sharp turn and went back under the stairwell. There, to Nella's surprise, was another door that was concealed from anyone who didn't know it was there. Taking another key from a nail, Sam opened the door and flipped on a light switch.

In front of them was a long, narrow room, approximately eight feet wide and twenty to thirty feet long. The room was lined with shelves on both sides. The shelves were loaded with jars of canned and dried food.

"See. We have enough food here to last us at least a year, and probably longer. So I don't think we have to be worried about getting snowbound. In fact, we probably could stay up here for several years and not run out of food. You want to try and see how long we could stay?"

The teasing note in his voice brought Nella's eyes from the awesome sight of the food, quickly to his. He was standing close, still holding Jake in his arms.

What would it be like to stay here for several years with just the three of them, she wondered? And what on earth had come over Sam? Why was he making all of these insinuating remarks all of a sudden?

"Go on, look around," he encouraged her.

Nella walked the length of the shelves and could not believe the variety of canned foods she saw. There was canned beef, pork, and chicken, and practically every kind of vegetable that could be grown in the area. Corn, peas, beans, tomatoes, onions, carrots — and the list went on. There were also jars containing dried peas and beans, and a few things she didn't recognize.

"Did you do all of this?" she asked, making her way back to him.

"No, not exactly. I have an arrangement with one of the neighbors, Mr. and Mrs. Adams. They weren't at the McCoys' house the other night. I hoped they would be, so you could meet them. They were good friends with my grandparents. Anyway, I buy all of the seeds to plant, furnish the tractor and gas, and they grow the food and prepare it, and we split it. This arrangement helps them, and me. They keep half and bring half over here. They have a key to the house, so they can bring the stuff in and keep it rotated so it doesn't get too old on the shelves. They also keep a watch on the house, year round."

Nella was almost back to Sam and Jake when she stopped and gave a blood-curdling scream.

"Nella, what's wrong?" Sam rushed toward her.

"No! Stop, Sam! Don't come any closer!" she warned, pointing at a huge spider hanging from a web, directly between them. She shivered uncontrollably as she looked at the ugly spider. She'd almost run her face right into it. The spider's body was the size of the ball of Nella's thumb. Just the thought of that thing being on her gave her cold chills.

Spotting the cause of her alarm, Sam burst out laughing. He gripped the web just above the spider and lowered the offending object to the floor, then kicked it under one of the shelves.

Nella looked at him in open-eyed horror. "Why didn't you kill it?"

"Because she'll eat other bugs that come in here to try to eat our food," Sam explained, as if talking to a child.

"Well, there's plenty of food in here to share with a few little bugs, and if that monster stays, I go," Nella said flatly, and started to push past Sam.

He reached out and stopped her with an arm across her waist.

"You really amaze me. You'll fight a stranger to protect my son. You'll risk your life in the ocean to save his life. You'll take on the world to stand up for what you believe in, but you're afraid of, no, horrified, of a *spider?*"

With Sam this close and those golden brown eyes staring deeply into hers, the spider seemed far away, and of minor importance.

"You gonna kiss her, or not?" Jake's small, impatient voice interrupted the moment.

"Yes, Son, I'm gonna kiss her." And he slowly lowered his lips to hers.

Nella couldn't have moved if she'd wanted to, as his eyes held her transfixed until his lips covered hers. The kiss was slow and gentle and probing, and would have gone on longer if Jake hadn't wrapped his arms around both of their necks and started giggling and trying to kiss each one of them on the cheek.

Sam and Nella started smiling even as their lips tried to hold the kiss, but the small boy was so persistent that Sam raised his head slowly. The smile was still on Nella's lips and her eyes were a soft, smoky haze as she opened them.

Sam wanted nothing more than to continue what he'd started, but Jake's voice interrupted his intentions. "Are you going to town now, Daddy?" The child had remembered the snow, and wanted to go play in it.

"Yes, I guess I'd better go, before it gets any later." Reluctantly, he led them back upstairs.

Sam left shortly thereafter and headed for Bowling Green, saying it would probably be at least two hours before he could get back.

The sun had been shining a little when he left, but the clouds soon moved back in, and now a few new flakes of snow were beginning to fall. Nella sat and watched it in awe. The serenity and beauty of it thrilled her.

Jake had become tired of waiting for his dad to return and had fallen asleep, so the house was quiet. Nella had time to herself, and as always of late, her thoughts went back to Sam. She just couldn't figure out where his change of attitude had come from, but ever since they spent the night with the McCoys' he'd acted differently toward her.

Was he just toying with her? He seemed so sincere, though. And he *was* different up here. Sam du Cannon the business magnate had become Sam du Cannon the laid-back, relaxed family man. And with that change came all the attention he was giving her lately.

What should she do? She was attracted to him, but was that all it was — just attraction?

She needed to fall in love with her husband like she needed a hole in her head. She knew she should try to discourage the attention she was getting from him, but she didn't want to. She enjoyed every moment of it, even if Sam wasn't sincere. But where would it lead? Would she fall in love with him only to be hurt when they returned to their other life and Sam became his old self?

Now, wait! She mentally shook herself. She was a strong woman, and in total control of her emotions. She wouldn't allow herself to fall in love with him, but why not play his game and see where he was going with it? If he was indeed just toying with her, just to add another woman to his long list, she could play that game, too. In fact, she could play that game better than the infallible Mr. Sam du Cannon. And he might be the one who fell in love with her against *his* will. Now wouldn't that be a hoot? How would Sam be if he were in love?

She smiled softly to herself as she made plans to charm and captivate the powerful Samuel L. du Cannon.

Sam realized a smile was playing with the corners of his mouth, and his eyes almost felt as if they were twinkling, as he maneuvered the Jeep up the last incline to the house. Surprised, he wondered how long it'd been since he felt like this. He was almost home, and couldn't wait to get there. Couldn't wait to be with his son, and the woman who waited for him there.

Woman. What a perfect description for Nella. He'd known many women in his thirty-five years, but none of them epitomized that word like Nella. She was *woman*.

At that thought he chuckled out loud and brought the Jeep to a stop in front of the house. He'd been listening to the radio all afternoon, and the cold front that was supposed to have missed them was coming straight at them. An Arctic mass of cold air was dipping lower south than it usually did this time of year. The weather forecasters were saying it could be the worst storm for this area in many years. Maybe even a record. But Sam didn't care. He was home, he had plenty of food, and he had a family. The warm glow in his inner being could keep them all warm for months.

Nella met him at the door and took some of the packages.

"Did you buy out Bowling Green?" she asked, as he went back to the Jeep for more packages.

"Just about," he said, "but a good man has to provide fer his fambly." He jokingly reverted to his "country" slang. "What's that heavenly smell?" he asked, coming through the door.

"Well," Nella joined in his game, "a good woman has ter keep 'er man fed, whilst he's out providin' fer her and the young'uns. That there smell is a pot of beef stew I made fer ye."

Laughing out loud together seemed so right. So natural. But suddenly serious, Sam handed Nella several of the bags.

"I took a chance and bought you some warm clothes, too. I hope they fit. The lady at the store was more than glad to help me." Satisfaction sounded in his voice.

Nella had an instant vision of a size six salesperson falling all over herself trying to help Sam decide what size clothes to buy for her.

As if reading her mind, Sam continued, "The sales lady is about your size, and very attractive. She had some great suggestions that helped me a lot." Then, stopping and looking Nella up and down, he grinned. "But her boobs weren't nearly as big as yours are."

"Sam!" Nella scolded. Then, remembering she was going to play along with him, she batted her eyelashes at him and said in her best Scarlet O'Hara drawl, "Why, thank you, suh."

Caught off guard, Sam headed toward her, but she darted behind the couch for protection.

"Leave me alone! I want to see my new clothes!"

She was amazed at what she found. He'd bought a beautiful wool cape, boots, socks, several pair of jeans, and pullover sweaters.

"Sam, you act like we're going to be here all winter," Nella protested.

"Well, according to the weather men, we might."

Nella hadn't bothered trying to hear a weather forecast, so she was surprised to hear Sam saying they were in for a bad storm. "Are we going to be okay?" Concern edged her voice.

"We're going to be fine," Sam assured her. "In fact, this is going to be the best winter I've had in years. I hope you'll feel the same way." Not giving her a chance to answer, he left the room, saying over his shoulder, "Go put on some warm clothes while I wake Jake up. I want to play in the snow."

Nella hastily dressed in a pair of the jeans and a pretty purple sweater, and put on her new boots. She was surprised at how well everything fit. Sam and the sales lady had done an excellent job of fitting her.

By the time she'd dressed Jake was awake, and Sam had him in a new pair of jeans, a hooded sweatshirt, and a fleece-lined, water-resistant jacket. Jake was strutting around the room. "Look at my new clothes! Can I sleep in them tonight?"

"Well, I think after the snow gets them all cold and wet, you won't want to sleep in them, Son," Sam told him patiently, and then looked at Nella. "Wow! I did pretty good, huh?"

"Well, the sweater could have been a little larger," Nella answered, pulling at it to try to stretch it a little.

"Oh, I like it just like it is," Sam said with a lopsided grin. "I like it a lot." He gave a knowing wink.

Before she could answer, Jake tugged at her hand. "Come on, I want to go outside!"

The snow was coming down harder now, and the flakes were huge and fluffy. Nella stopped and stood with her face turned up into the falling snow. She delighted in the feel of it landing on her skin. It was so quiet, and smelled so fresh. She felt she could stand here forever and become a snow queen. She'd always loved the beach, but she'd found a new love.

Jake was running and jumping and falling in the snow. He'd never seen snow before, and his excitement was complete.

Nella was still standing motionless, looking around her in awe, when she felt the whop of a snowball on the back of her head. She turned around to catch Sam in the act of throwing a second snowball. Just as she looked at him a large snowball hit her right in the face.

The snow stung when it hit her and she immediately grabbed her face with both hands, bending forward to brush the snow off. Then the idea came. She dropped to her knees, bent forward, and moaned softly.

Sam was beside her instantly, leaning over her. "Nella, I'm sorry! I didn't mean to hit you in the face." The concern in his voice almost made Nella change her plan, but not quite. She reached out suddenly and grabbed him around the legs. Pushing all her weight against him, she shoved him backwards into the snow, causing him to land flat on his back. Moving swiftly, she straddled him and started scooping hands full of snow into his face.

Laughing heartily, Jake joined her. The surprised look on Sam's face was priceless. Then he started laughing and trying to get up.

Nella knew she was in for some horrible punishment when he did get up, so she jumped swiftly to her feet and ran away as fast as the deepening snow would allow.

When she stopped to look back, Sam was casually helping Jake start a snowman. He acted as if nothing had happened. Oh no. Now she'd have to be constantly on guard, because she knew Sam would get even. The question was when and how?

Moving a little closer, she called. "We're even, okay? You hit me two times, and I only rolled you once. That makes us even, okay?" No answer. Not even a hint that he'd heard her. He just continued talking to Jake.

"Sam? Did you hear me?" She moved a little closer, but he continued to ignore her.

Jake called, "Mommy, come and help us! We're gonna make a really big snowman."

"Sam, we're even, okay? Promise!" Now she was even closer, and when Sam didn't answer her, she stamped her foot angrily. "Sam! Answer me!"

The foot that she stamped landed on a slick, frozen spot on the ground, causing her to lose her footing, and before she knew what was happening she was lying flat on her back. As swiftly as a springing jungle cat, Sam was on top of her.

But he wasn't straddling her like she had been him. He was lying almost full-length on her. His face was very close to hers and she could feel his breath warm her skin. His hands held each side of her face.

"So you want to play dirty, huh?" His eyes glinted with mischief.

Now he had both hands full of her hair, and she couldn't turn her head to either side, even if she'd wanted to. Lowering his head only slightly, he kissed one corner of her mouth, then the other. Without parting his lips, he gently brushed back and forth across hers. Then, parting his lips only slightly, he nibbled at her full bottom lip.

Nella had never experienced the sensations that were charging through her body. Her lower stomach was churning with feelings she had never felt with Nick.

"Sam?" She opened her lips to whisper his name, and when she did, he gently traced her mouth with his tongue. He was driving her crazy. She could feel her entire body going limp with desire. Her heart was pounding so hard her chest ached. He moved a hand down to cup a breast as his lips fully claimed hers.

Vaguely, they both became aware of Jake crying. In unison, as if in slow motion, they turned their dazed eyes in his direction to find him staring at a collapsed snowman.

"Daddy! Help me!" Jake pleaded.

Sam slowly raised himself from Nella.

"We'll continue this later," he promised, as he went to help Jake repair the fallen snowman.

Chapter 10

Sam volunteered to clean up the kitchen while Nella got Jake ready for bed. He knew he should be confronting a lot of questions that were trying to surface, but he didn't want to deal with anything, at this point, that might interfere with the new happiness he felt.

He hadn't felt this content, this happy — that silly grin was coming back on his face. He almost used the word "giddy" when trying to describe how he was feeling. He hadn't felt like this since he was a child. He felt like a teenager, falling in love for the first time.

Maybe he *was* falling in love for the first time. The thought stopped him dead still.

Love? Could that be what was happening to him? He knew he hadn't been in love with Vanessa when they married. Getting married just seemed the socially correct thing to do at the time. He also knew he'd never been truly in love. In fact, he hadn't thought he was capable of loving a woman.

The women he'd known were all shallow, and interested mostly in his money. Over the years he'd developed a callousness toward women in general, and lumped them all in his own little "love them and leave them" category.

Then came Nella. Gentle, yet strong. Soft, loving, alluring, and, he was beginning to realize, very sexy, Nella. Her smoky blue eyes were beautiful. And that sensual mouth. He could picture that mouth —

"Sam, you need some help finishing up?" Her voice from the doorway startled him back to reality.

"No, I'm almost finished," he answered, without turning around. He'd become partially aroused, just thinking about her.

Nella went into the living room and stood looking out the window. Was she headed for a broken heart? She was definitely not a love 'em and leave 'em type, so the fact that she was considering making love with Sam made her know her emotions had advanced farther than she cared to deal with at this moment. Especially if she were going to continue her plan of getting to him before he got to her. She sure hoped she didn't get caught in her own trap.

Sam came up behind her and slipped his arms around her waist. She could feel the warmth of his entire body pressed against her back. He rested his chin on her shoulder, his face pressed against hers.

Together they stood silently watching the falling snow. Words didn't seem necessary, as their thoughts were joined.

The ringing phone startled them back to reality. Reluctantly, Sam walked to the phone and lifted the receiver to his ear.

"Hello — No, I haven't heard the weather tonight — Are you serious? No, we have everything we need, as far as I know — Okay, thank you for calling. Yes, I'll let you know if we need anything."

Replacing the phone, Sam turned to Nella with a slightly concerned look on his face.

"What?" she asked impatiently.

"We're going to be snowbound. That was Mr. Adams, and he says the weather forecasters are saying this could be the worst storm to hit this area in forty years. We could be snowed in for several weeks." As he talked, he walked across the room to turn the television on. Every channel was covering the weather, and saying the same thing.

Nella knew she should be concerned, but in this house with Sam, who always seemed so much in charge, she felt no fear. In fact, it was almost a comforting feeling to know they couldn't go back to their other world for a while. And no one could get to them. A soft smile toyed with the corners of her mouth as she thought of the cozy aspects of being snowbound with Sam du Cannon, now that her feelings were changing toward him.

Slowly she became aware that Sam stood staring at her.

"What?" she asked.

"Aren't you going into hysterics or start demanding that we get airlifted out, or something typically female like that?"

"Sam," she said, in a condescending voice. "You really do disappoint me. Number one, that was a totally chauvinistic thing to say, and number two, you've known me long enough to know that I don't do many things that are 'typically female.'"

"You mean you're not concerned at all about being snowbound up here for an undetermined length of time?"

"Well, as you showed me earlier, we have plenty of food, and heat, so why would I be concerned? This will be a new experience for me. We'll make the best of the situation, and try to have a lot of fun. Are you worried?" She turned the question back to him.

Suddenly a smile covered his entire face.

"If we live together for fifty years, will you still continue to surprise me?"

The question took them both by surprise.

"I'll try," Nella whispered, for lack of a better answer. She had never thought of living with Sam for that many years.

He clicked the TV off and came slowly toward her. Taking her by the hand, he led her to the couch and they sat down. He switched the lamp off. The only light in the room came from what drifted in from the light above the stove in the kitchen. They could see the falling snow through the sliding glass door. Sam still held her hand in his.

"When I was a teenager, I had romantic fantasies about being caught in a snowstorm with a beautiful woman, and we had all the time we needed to make love over and over, with no interruptions. The only time I've ever been snowbound with a woman before now was with Vanessa, and she went into a bitch fit that lasted the entire week we were here. We didn't make love once. In fact, Vanessa and I never 'made love.' We had sex, but we never really made love. There's a difference, you know." There was a sadness in his voice that Nella had never heard before.

All of a sudden she wanted to be that girl from his teenage fantasy. She wanted to show him how loving a woman could really be. She wanted to let him know that she did know the difference between having sex and making slow, gentle, long-lasting love.

Reaching up, she pulled his head down to her. Her lips found his and she started slowly, sensually kissing him. His response was automatic as he drew her into his arms and deepened the kiss.

Before the kiss went too far, Nella pulled back and reached up and started unbuttoning his shirt. She wanted to feel his skin touching hers. As she undid each button, she kissed the open spot that was exposed. She heard the low moan that escaped Sam's throat as she made her way down to the last button. She pulled the shirt apart and placed her open hands on his chest, to feel the warmth and strength that came from him.

Sam reached down and grasped the bottom of the sweater she had on, slipping it over her head. Then, slowly, he unhooked the back of her bra and removed it, to reveal her breasts to his hungry eyes. As he gently took them both in his hands, Nella leaned into him. A wave of pure ecstasy engulfed her as his hands worked their magic.

But instead of losing control and letting him do all the work, she again took the lead. Leaning over, she placed her mouth over one of his nipples and gently nipped it with her teeth. She heard his sharp in-drawn breath and wondered if she was the first woman who'd ever introduced him to this pleasure. She teased the hardening nipple with her tongue and teeth, then moved her sweet torment to the other nipple to give it equal time.

"You're driving me crazy," he groaned hoarsely.

"That's my plan," she whispered back.

Nella kissed her way down his stomach, stopping to give his deep navel special attention with her tongue. She could feel his arousal against her body. Her breasts rubbed against his clothing, teasing her tender nipples, giving her as much delight as she was giving him. She slowly undid his belt and pants, to expose his excitement.

Sam, knowing he was too close to losing control prematurely, caught Nella's hand, which was driving him crazy, and pulled her back up to him. Then together, in mutual consent, they slid off the couch onto the soft Persian rug on the floor.

Now Sam was the one in charge. He kissed her hungrily, as if he'd never get enough of the feel of her soft, full lips. He traced kisses down her throat and nibbled at her breasts. He took long, gentle pleasure with her peaks and went repeatedly from one to the other, until Nella thought she'd go crazy from wanting him. Finally, he entered her, and together they reached that final crest at the same time. It was a moment they both knew was different than any either of them had experienced before.

They made love several times that night. Each time seemed better than before. Sam was in awe that his fantasy was finally coming true, and Nella was making sure he'd never forget this time they spent together, even if he tried.

Sometimes during the night, they wound up in Sam's bed.

Slowly, Nella came awake and opened her eyes to look directly into Jake's questioning gaze. His chin rested in his hands as he leaned onto the bed and stared at her.

"Whatcha doing in here?" he asked. "I went to get in bed with you, and you weren't in your bed. Now here you are in Daddy's bed."

Nella realized Sam was still asleep, so she whispered to Jake to be quiet, then gathered him into the bed beside her and wrapped her arms around him. He giggled and snuggled in as close as he could get.

This was true happiness, Nella decided as she drifted back to sleep, her arms wrapped tightly around him.

Sam came awake gradually. He realized his body spooned Nella's perfectly. His right arm was around her waist and his face was half buried in her hair. As he remembered the night of pleasure they'd just spent, he automatically reached up and gently massaged one of her breasts.

"Stop that, Daddy!" Jake's small voice scolded, as he pushed Sam's hand away from Nella's breast.

"Oh, hell!" Surprise registered in Sam's voice. "How long has he been in bed with us?" he whispered into Nella's hair.

Nella had only dozed on and off after Jake got in bed with them. It was obvious the child's sleep was over, but it felt so good to lie here with Sam's arm around her. She was afraid if she moved, the night they'd just spent would become a memory, not to be repeated.

"About an hour," she said.

"Well, how am I supposed to proceed with the plan I had in mind?" His voice was husky from sleep and emotion.

"Oh, we'll find a way," she promised, wiggling her bottom seductively against his arousal.

Jake, ready for his day to begin, sprang from the bed. "Come on, Mommy. I'm hungry." He pulled on Nella's hand.

Sam's moan was genuine as he reluctantly let Nella leave the bed. Her laughter followed her from the room.

When Sam joined them in the kitchen, Jake was contentedly eating a bowl of oatmeal.

Closing the refrigerator door, Nella turned to Sam as she heard him enter the room.

"You know, the only thing that concerns me about this situation is milk. We only have a gallon left, and Jake's really going to miss his milk."

"I don't think that'll be a real problem," Sam answered, going to the door. A blast of cold air greeted them as he stooped down and picked something up. Closing the door, he handed Nella a gallon jar of ice-cold milk.

"What on earth?" She took the milk and looked at Sam in disbelief.

"The Allens have several milk cows. They always have fresh milk, butter, and cheese. Mr. Allen knew we'd need milk with a child up here."

"But how did he get it up here? And why isn't it frozen?" The snow was still falling heavily, and the temperature had to be well below freezing.

"Come here." Sam motioned Nella to the window. "See those tracks out there?"

Nella saw the deep grooves in the snow, and nodded her head.

"Mr. Allen has a sleigh and an old mule named Fred who can travel these hills like a mountain goat. All Mr. Allen needs to do is hitch Fred to the sleigh and he can go just about anywhere he wants to, in practically any kind of weather."

"Then we really aren't snowbound," Nella mused. "Mr. Allen could rescue us any time we needed."

"Yes, that's true." Sam was standing close and looking deeply into Nella's eyes.

"Then why did you let me believe we were up here with no help?" Nella almost felt angry.

"Partly because I wanted to see your reaction, and partly, and I guess mostly, because I was afraid you'd want to leave if you thought you could." His voice was so sincere that the irritation Nella felt disappeared.

"And you really wanted to sit this storm out, didn't you?" Her voice was soft and understanding.

"Yes."

"Sam, if you love this place so much, why haven't you spent more time here?"

"I've been asking myself that a lot these last few days." He paused a moment, then continued. "So you aren't angry with me for not being more honest with you?"

"I really should be, but no, I don't guess I am." Nella tried to look stern, but couldn't keep the smile from starting on her lips.

He leaned down and kissed her gently. It was a different kiss. It was a warm and companionable kiss. It was a kiss of gratitude for her understanding. And it was a frightening kiss.

The other kisses they had shared were lustful, sensual kisses that aroused her body, but this one touched, seared, and branded her heart, and she knew she was in trouble.

Later, after lunch, Jake crawled up on the sofa to watch cartoons and was soon asleep.

Nella went to Sam's office. His door was open, but it was obvious he was busy working. She was trying to decide whether to disturb him or not when he sensed her presence and looked up.

"Come on in," he invited.

"Well, I didn't mean to bother you, but Jake's asleep."

"Oh?" He tried to look as if he didn't understand why she was telling him this, but didn't quite hide the flash of his eyes.

"Uh huh," Nella said softly, "and I thought you might want to finish what you tried to start this morning."

"This morning?" He pretended not to remember.

"Uh huh," Nella repeated, coming to him. She started slowly unbuttoning her blouse.

"Yes, I think I'm beginning to remember a little." His husky voice belied the game he was playing.

Nella placed her hands on each side of his head and pulled him to her. She drew his face close enough that his lips were touching one of her nipples. She slightly moved her breast, causing his lips to open, and she could feel his hot breath through the material of her bra.

Not being able to hold out any longer, Sam opened his mouth to playfully nip and tease her nipple though the lace of her bra.

Laughing softly, Nella said, "I believe you just regained your memory, Mr. du Cannon."

Reaching behind her, Nella undid the hooks on her bra to let her breasts free for Sam's eager touch. She slowly and sensually unfastened Sam's pants, and freed him so she would have enough access to give him pleasure. She placed her hands on his shoulders and playfully teased his mouth with her breasts, then straddled his lap and captured what he so willingly offered.

Later, as they lay exhausted from making love, Sam said, "You are, without a doubt, the most passionate woman I've ever known. And you turn me on more than any woman ever has."

Not knowing what to say, Nella just reached up and lightly kissed him. "You ain't seen nothing yet," she whispered.

Soon they both drifted into a contented sleep.

Nella woke first. She lay quietly and watched Sam sleep. He truly was a beautiful man. In sleep, his chiseled features softened to become almost boyish. As she lay watching him his eyes drifted languidly open, as if he sensed she was memorizing his face.

Embarrassed she had been caught, her own face blushed soft pink.

He reached over and gently brushed her cheek with the back of his fingers. "Lady, you must be having some very naughty thoughts, if getting caught looking at me makes you blush like that." His hand trailed down to encircle her neck.

"I was not!" she denied too quickly. "I was thinking you look like a little boy when you're asleep."

"Well, I'm afraid this little boy is having some very big boy thoughts," he said, reaching for her.

"Sam," she protested with fake consternation. "You're going to wear yourself out."

"Not this time. I'm going to let you do all the work for a change."

Knowing exactly what he wanted, Nella slowly and carefully mounted him. She reveled in the excitement the position was giving her, and again, together they reached the pinnacle that only two people lost in pleasing each other can reach.

Eventually they lay flat on their backs, eyes closed, once again exhausted.

"My fantasy was never this good," Sam whispered.

Mission partly accomplished, Nella thought, but only smiled and said, "Hmmm."

The sharp ringing of the phone broke their spell. Sam answered, and Nella could tell it was business, so she got up and headed for the shower.

Several days later, Sam came from his office, where he'd been on the phone again.

"Next week is Thanksgiving, and the Adams want us to come spend the holiday with them. Mr. Adams will come and get us on the sleigh, and they want us to stay a few days. What do you think?"

It would be the first time they'd left the house since their visit to Tommy and Amy's. The chance to get away briefly was kind of exciting to Nella. The heavy snow had slowed down and now they were only having occasional flurries, but they'd had fourteen inches, altogether, with drifts much deeper.

"If you think it's safe to try, I'd enjoy visiting for a few days." She gave Sam the answer he was hoping for.

"We'll be okay if it doesn't snow any more than it's doing right now. If it should come a heavier snow between now and then, I don't think we should try it."

Nella had to take his word for it, as she didn't know how sleighs worked, but she sure felt sorry for the animal who had to pull them through the heavy snow.

She couldn't believe they'd been here on the mountain for as long as they had. And she was still in awe of the transformation in Sam. His lovemaking was so gentle at times it made her throat ache just to think of it. Yet at other times there was an urgency that almost frightened her. It was as if he were afraid their time was running out, and it would all be over soon.

They spent the following week in anticipation of the pending visit. Mrs. Adams had told them not to bring any food, but at Nella's insistence Sam agreed to let her bake a cake and some pies, "just to help out," Nella said.

That actually pleased Sam, because it was a custom of the area to always bring something when visiting someone, and he knew it'd make a good impression on the Adams.

It was late Tuesday afternoon. Mr. Adams was supposed to pick them up on Wednesday afternoon. Nella was in the kitchen finishing up her last pie. Jake was taking his mid-afternoon nap, and Sam was in his office doing paperwork.

Nella stepped inside the pantry to put away the things she'd been using to make the pie. As she reached over her head to put away the last ingredient, she felt Sam's hands slip around her from behind. They skillfully made their way under her loose sweater to capture a breast in each hand.

He drew her back against him and started kissing the back of her neck. As he kneaded her breasts, he kissed his way slowly toward her mouth, and she turned her head to give him full access to her lips. She could feel his arousal start as she leaned back into him.

"You have enchanted me, woman. I can't think about anything except making love to you," he whispered against her upturned mouth.

"Is that a bad thing?" she asked, in a weakened voice.

"Not a bad thing, but a highly unusual thing. I'm not usually this captivated by a woman," he admitted, tracing her bottom lip with the ball of his thumb.

"Well, what do we need to do about it?" she asked, slowly draw-ing his thumb into her mouth.

"Oh, I do have a temporary solution," he promised, and pro-ceeded to reveal to her what it was.

Afterward they stood holding each other, weak from exhaustion. No words were spoken. No words were needed. But both knew that eventually they'd have to discuss what was developing between them.

That night, as they sat on the couch and watched the evening news, waiting to see the weather report, the announcer said, "Today, charges were filed against the nationally known Samuel L. du Cannon by Miranda Smythe, for child support for her unborn child. According to Ms. Smythe, Sam du Cannon, the food chain mogul, disappeared into thin air after he found out she was pregnant with his child."

As she felt the color drain from her face, Nella remembered her walk on the beach back in Hawaii, and the part of Sam and Miranda's conversation that she didn't hear before they reached her. Was that the reason Miranda was so upset when Sam refused to continue seeing her? Did he know she was pregnant then, and just didn't want to acknowledge it?

The announcer continued, "Miranda Smythe urges Sam du Cannon to take immediate action and contact her so they can come to an agreement about a settlement."

The camera flashed a shot of Miranda with John McHill as her escort. There were a few brief shots of old film footage of Sam.

Sam snapped off the TV with the remote control. His face was dark with anger. "Well, I wondered how and when it would come, but I never expected this." His voice was low and tinged with fury.

Nella wanted desperately to ask him if Miranda were pregnant with his child, but instinct told her it was not the time to ask that question.

Making his decision quickly, Sam turned to Nella. "You know I have to go and fight this thing. Miranda and John have somehow joined forces with my in-laws, and are waging a battle against me. I have to go and fight them. I want you and Jake to go ahead to the Adams' house for Thanksgiving, but I have to go and get to the bottom of this."

"No." Quiet determination sounded in her voice.

"No? No, what?" Sam stopped his troubled pacing to look at Nella.

"I don't want to go to the Adams' without you. They're strangers to me. I know they're good people, but I don't want to go alone. I want to go with you."

"Nella, that's not possible. I won't be able to catch a flight out of here. I'll have to get Mr. Adams to come up here and get me, and then I'll have to rent a vehicle and drive. That won't be safe for you and Jake."

"But it is safe for you?"

"I'll be able to take care of myself."

"Why do you have to go? Why can't your lawyers just take care of the situation?" She was beginning to wonder if he wanted to go to Miranda.

As if reading her mind, Sam came over and sat beside her, placing his arm around her shoulders. "Nella, if Miranda is pregnant, and she sure didn't look it, the child couldn't possibly be mine. I did go to bed with her once, but that was right after Vanessa died. If Miranda is pregnant with my child, she's about two months past due."

Again Nella had a flashback of the beach, and how upset Miranda was because Sam wouldn't see her again. Could that have been part of a scheme that was being planned even at that time?

"You do believe me, don't you?" Sam's eyes pleaded for understanding.

"Yes, I believe you." She couldn't let him know she'd overheard them on the beach.

"So you'll stay at the Adams' place?"

"No. I'll stay here. Jake and I will be fine."

"But I'll feel a lot better about you if I know you're with them."

"Sam, don't you know how restless small children get when they aren't in their own surroundings? Jake will be miserable, and so will I. Having to cope with him, plus having to be with total strangers, and not knowing when you'll be back — no, I just don't want to do it."

Sam could tell her mind was made up. "Okay," he gave in reluctantly. He called the Adams and told them the bad news, and made arrangements for Mr. Adams to pick him up the next morning in the sleigh and take him down to Bowling Green.

He went over every possible detail with Nella, drilling her on things to do in case of an emergency. He showed her how to stoke the furnace. He made sure she knew where the oil lamps and candles were in case the electricity went off, and made her promise again that she'd call the Adams if anything at all went wrong.

When they finally went to bed, Sam pulled Nella close. He didn't make love to her, he just held her tightly. Each time she woke up during the night he was still holding onto her, as if he needed all the strength he could draw from her for the upcoming battle.

As for Nella, she felt a tinge of fear settling in the pit of her stomach. Would this be the end of what they'd shared here? Would he go back to his other world and realize how much he'd missed it, and not want to come back to her and what they'd been sharing?

Her night was filled with unanswered questions and fitful sleep.

Much as she had feared, upon rising the next morning, Sam had reverted to the man she'd met and married. He was crisp and businesslike, absorbed in his preparations for the trip and mentally gearing up for what lay ahead.

When Mr. Adams arrived, Sam gathered Jake into his arms and held him tightly against his chest. His eyes glistened with tears as he promised, "Daddy will be back soon, and everything is going to be okay." He hadn't wanted Jake to know where he was going. He didn't want the child to worry about something that he damn well wasn't going to let happen.

Turning to Nella, he placed his hands on each side of her face and kissed her gently. "No matter what you hear and see on the news, hang on to what we've had here. Nothing else is real. No matter how nasty it gets, don't believe it. Promise me that."

"I promise," Nella whispered, and the tinge of fear she had felt all night became a knot in the pit of her stomach.

Chapter 11

As Nella watched Sam disappear around the bend, a loneliness settled over her that she had never experienced before, not even when she walked away from her beloved father's grave on the day he was buried.

She knew Sam would be back. He had to come back for Jake, and for her.

Yes, he'd come back *for* her — but would he come back *to* her? Again the nagging questions came. Had he only made love to her because he needed a woman, and she was the only one around?

Without conscious thought of doing so, she wound up on the couch with Jake clutched closely in her arms.

Why was she so upset? She knew she wasn't afraid to stay here alone. That wasn't the reason for this crushing pain in her chest, the feeling someone was ripping her heart out.

"I love my daddy," Jake whispered, sensing that Nella was upset, but not knowing how to comfort her.

"I love your daddy, too, Jake," Nella whispered against his soft, little-boy hair.

And then she knew.

The realization came like an explosion. She was caught in her own trap! She'd known it was a dangerous game when she first set out to make Sam love her in spite of his statements that it would never happen. She'd known the attraction she felt for him could backfire on her, and now she knew she was in love with him. Not with the Sam du Cannon she'd met and married, but the Sam du Cannon she'd come to know up here on this mountaintop. The Sam du Cannon who was warm and gentle and loving.

She knew her life would never be the same. But instead of the despondency she should have felt for making such a mess of her life, she suddenly felt exhilarated.

"I love him!" she repeated, but this time more loudly.

Jake raised his head from her shoulder and looked at her with wide, inquiring eyes.

It felt so good to admit it. It felt so good to say it. A thrill of excitement filled her being. How *good* it felt to be in love.

Sam would win the battle for the custody of Jake. She had no doubts about that. And he'd come back for them. And if he didn't love her now, she'd make sure he did before she was finished. She would see to it.

"Mommy, you're silly," giggled Jake.

"No, Darling, Mommy's giddy!" she answered, squeezing him tightly.

As Mr. Adams laboriously guided the old mule and sleigh back down the winding road toward Bowling Green, Sam sat quietly trying to sort out his feelings.

He wasn't aware of the beauty of the winter wonderland around them, nor did he seem to notice when, occasionally, the mule would slightly slip on the ice and fight to regain his footing, or when the sleigh would get precariously close to the edge of one of the deep ravines that dropped away from each side of the road.

He only grunted halfheartedly to the occasional comments the older man made, so Mr. Adams finally gave up trying to talk to him and concentrated on getting them to their destination safely.

Sam reflected over his good-bye to Nella. He'd been surprised at his automatic urge to tell her he loved her. He'd been dumbfounded when the unexpected words had leaped to his tongue. But he'd held back and hadn't said them.

What was going on here? Was his subconscious trying to tell him something? Did he love her? Or was it just the trauma of leaving her and Jake alone during conditions like this? Would he get back into his other world and be bombarded with the same old routine and reactions as before?

Did he love her? The nagging question kept popping up.

Yes, a quiet voice answered, unsummoned, from the innermost depth of his being.

Suddenly his laughter rang out into the quietness of the snow covered world around them, causing the old mule's ears to twitch and the old man to jump.

"Yes!" he said aloud. "Yes, yes, yes!"

Mr. Adams looked at him as if he'd taken leave of his senses.

"Mr. Adams, I've just made a discovery that will change my life." He didn't go into detail, and the other man didn't ask.

Two nights later, Sam called Nella. He told her briefly about his trip and that he'd had no problems getting back to Charleston. But Nella could hear the concern in his voice when he asked how she and Jake were coping. Were they warm? Had the furnace given them any problems? Was the electricity still on?

"Sam," Nella finally interrupted him, "we're fine. Really, we are."

"You know you can call the Adams anytime," Sam repeated the obvious.

"I know. Mrs. Adams called and tried to get us to come down and made me promise I'd call if I had any trouble. I promised her I would, and I promise you I'll call them if anything at all comes up. Okay?"

He seemed a little more relaxed now, and after talking a little longer to her, then to Jake, he reluctantly hung up the phone.

He'd sounded different to Nella. She couldn't quite put her finger on the reason. He was abrupt and businesslike as he used to be, but his voice definitely had a different sound to it. Was someone there with him? Had he gotten back and changed his mind about Miranda?

"Stop it!" she reprimanded herself aloud. But she couldn't shake the feeling Sam had wanted to say more. That he was about to say something, but had held himself back. The feeling stayed with her long after she put Jake to bed and sat staring at the muted TV, her heart full and hurting from missing Sam.

Sam slowly hung the receiver up. He ached with longing to be back in Kentucky with Nella and Jake.

He had come so close to telling her of his newly discovered love, but for some reason he couldn't say the words. Why? Why couldn't he say, "I love you?"

Had he ever said those words to anyone?

The question came out of nowhere. But the more he tried to remember, the more he realized he didn't know the last time, or the last person, he had said those three little words to. Of course he said it to Jake, because Nella had taught Jake to say, "I love you," and naturally Sam's response was, "I love you, too, Son."

He'd never told Vanessa he loved her, because he didn't see any need to lie to her. They both knew why they'd gotten married, and love was not the reason.

He knew his grandparents loved him, but he couldn't remember them saying it. They just didn't verbally express their love — to each other or to him. But he never doubted they loved each other, or him.

His parents? Suddenly he had a dim memory of a shadowy figure leaning over him each night, kissing him and telling him that she loved him.

"I love you too, Mama," he whispered, as tears unexpectedly filled his eyes. And he knew that his mother, whom he had lost at such an early age, had been the last woman to whom he'd confessed his love.

Was that why it was so hard for him to love someone? Was he afraid he'd lose them like he'd lost his mother?

He was reaching for the phone to call Nella back when someone knocked on the door.

"Damn!" he muttered, as he went to see who could possibly know he was already in town. He would call Nella later, he promised himself as he answered the door.

"Hello, Sam." Miranda's voice dripped honey.

The fight was on.

Back on the mountain in Kentucky, Nella glanced at the phone number Sam had given her. Maybe she should call him.

She reached for the phone, and glanced at the clock. Eleven o'clock. He was probably already asleep, and she shouldn't disturb him.

With a heavy heart, she got up and went to bed.

A few days later as Nella sat and watched the weather report, she was delighted to hear that it was warming up. The snow and ice should start melting by the following day. Relief flooded through her. She had loved being snowbound with Sam, but being up here alone had caused her to feel more vulnerable than she'd admitted to Sam.

If the warmer weather held for a few days, she could drive Sam's Jeep down to Bowling Green and spend a few hours. The thought of being able to get out of the house thrilled her.

Jake looked up from his coloring book and asked, "Why are you happy, Mommy?" She hadn't realized until then that she was smiling.

"The snow is going to melt, and we can go to town in a couple of days," she explained to him.

"Can we see a movie?"

"Yes, that's a good idea, Jake. We'll shop a little, eat lunch, and then see a movie."

"Goodie!" Jake exclaimed, clapping his hands. Apparently he needed to get out of the house, too.

In Charleston, Sam was caught up in meetings with lawyers and the hearings he had to attend to fight the lawsuit Miranda had filed against him and his

business. As he suspected, his in-laws were involved with her, and so was John McHill.

As Sam was thrown together with Miranda in the hearings and watched her lie under oath about their love affair, saying it had continued even after his marriage to Nella, he wondered how he'd ever had the stomach to be intimate with her even once. He wondered how much his in-laws were paying her to follow through with this scheme.

She produced proof that she was approximately three months pregnant. Sam speculated the baby was John McHill's. He wondered if she actually thought he was too stupid to have blood tests done, if this farce proceeded much further.

Miranda's lawyers even produced pictures of Nella dancing at the company party in Hawaii. Whoever took the pictures was good, because each shot had caught Nella in a pose or look that seemed to appear as if she were flirting with every man there.

It infuriated Sam that they would try to make her appear unfit to care for Jake. He knew her behavior at the party had been innocent. His only regret was that he hadn't spent more time with her that night, instead of abandoning her like some jerk.

He had to fight constantly to keep his mind on what was being said. He kept thinking about going home and making love to Nella all night long. But he knew he had to stay here and win the fight, or the life he wanted so desperately to return to would not exist.

By Friday, the snow had melted enough that Nella felt safe in taking Jake and heading for Bowling Green. They had a wonderful day. They ate, they shopped, they saw a movie, and they even stopped by a small circus was set up in a parking lot.

When they got home there was a message on the answering machine from Sam.

Nella was so distraught that she had missed him that she automatically picked up the phone and called him, only to hear his answering machine come on. She left him a message that the snow had melted and how they had spent the day, and assured him they were fine.

Later that night, the phone rang and Nella ran to answer it. Her heart pounded in anticipation of hearing Sam's voice.

"Hello," she breathed expectantly into the receiver.

"My, my, you have a sexy voice," John McHill said from the other end of the line.

Stunned at hearing his voice, and disappointed that it wasn't Sam, Nella didn't speak for a few moments. A sudden thought filled her with panic. "What do you want? Is something wrong with Sam?"

"No, nothing's wrong with Sam. I'm just doing you a favor. The court ruled today that Jake's grandparents will get custody of him. I just wanted to let you know. They know where you are and they plan to fly up and get the kid on Monday."

"Why are you telling me this?"

"Because I like you and I know you have Jake's best interests at heart. I just thought you might want to know."

"Well, of course Sam will be with them when they come after Jake, won't he?" Panic and despair filled her at once. She was going to lose Jake, and in so doing she would lose Sam.

John McHill hung up the phone receiver and looked at Miranda. "I sure hope you know what you're doing. We could be in a lot of trouble if this backfires on us."

"Trust me, John, this is a foolproof plan."

Nella stared at the phone she had just hung up, then looked at Jake as he quietly sat and watched cartoons. She felt her heart slowly breaking. She would lose him, but the pain she felt was more for him than for herself. He'd made it plain on many occasions that he didn't like his grandmother. Now he'd be forced to live with her. His happiness as a child, and the way he would turn out as an adult, was truly at stake here.

How had this happened? How could any judge rule that Sam was an unfit parent? Unless — maybe there were things about him she didn't know.

No! She'd watched him with Jake over the past few months, and she knew he loved his son. And he was a wonderful father. No matter what his past had held, Nella knew Sam would always do the right thing toward Jake.

What was she going to do? She had to think of a way to keep those horrible people from taking Jake on Monday. If Sam just had a little more time, she knew he could turn this thing around.

"Look, Mommy," Jake interrupted her train of thought. "See all the water. That looks like our 'nother home where you lived."

"That's it!" Nella came alive. "Jake, you're brilliant! How would you like to go visit our other home?"

"But what if Daddy comes home and can't find us?"

"I'll let Daddy know where we are, but if anyone else calls on the phone, we mustn't tell them where we're going, okay? No one but Daddy gets to know. It's our secret, okay, Jake?"

"Okay, but why do we have a secret?" The question caught Nella by surprise.

"Well, because — uh, because we don't want anyone to know we're leaving this house empty." She knew her explanation was weak, but it seemed to satisfy Jake.

"When are we leaving?"

"Tomorrow, darling. Now let Mommy think."

The plan came swiftly and completely. She would pack their clothes tonight, and early in the morning she and Jake would get in the Jeep and head for South Carolina. Tomorrow was Saturday. By Monday she and Jake would be somewhere on the interstate, or maybe already there if the trip went smoothly.

She could feel excitement build as she made plans. It would take them a while to figure out where she was, and the added time would give Sam a chance to try to turn their situation around.

Without stopping to consider the possible consequences, Nella started packing their bags.

Before she went to bed, Nella called Sam's number, but the answering machine picked up again. Disappointed that he didn't answer, and wondering where he was, Nella reluctantly left a message. "Hi, Sam, it's Nella. John McHill called today and told me you'd lost custody of Jake. I just can't believe it.

"I'm taking him and going back to South Carolina. We won't be here Monday when they come to pick him up. Maybe this will give you a few days to come up with a solution on how to beat them in their dirty little games.

"Jake and I miss you. Don't worry, I'll take good care of him."

John McHill and Miranda high-fived each other as they taped Nella's message from the van they'd parked in an inconspicuous area just close enough to tap into Sam's phone line.

"Now, all we have to do is cut and splice this tape and make it say exactly what we want it to say, and it'll look like we have a kidnapping on our hands." Miranda's wicked smile made John McHill wonder why he'd ever gotten involved with the woman.

Exhausted from a long day of legalities and paper shuffling, Sam stumbled into his apartment. The day had gone well. Soon this whole mess would be over, and he and Nella and Jake could relax with the farce of a lawsuit far behind them.

His in-laws looked desperate today. They knew they were losing the case. It bothered him a little that he hadn't seen John and Miranda in the courtroom at all. Where were they? They were usually right there under foot.

He glanced at the clock. Seeing that it was one a.m., he decided to wait until the morning to call Nella. She'd be so happy to hear the good progress they were making. If Monday went well, the case would surely be finished by Tuesday at the latest.

Without even checking his messages, Sam stumbled to bed and was soon fast asleep.

Exhausted from the long, stressful week, and knowing the next day was Saturday, Sam slept straight through until nine o'clock the next morning. When he woke up, he made coffee, then headed for the phone to call Nella.

Realizing he had messages, he listened to them first. When Nella's voice came on, he smiled just to hear her. But as he listened to her message, he stared at the machine, dumbfounded.

He played the message again just to make sure he'd understood what she was saying, then jerked the receiver up and dialed the Kentucky number.

"Come on, baby, answer the phone," he pleaded, as the phone continued to ring. But the recorder came on, with his voice saying to leave a message.

"Damn!" he exploded. "Nella, if you're in the house, pick up the phone. Come on, honey, hear me. Pick up the phone. Jake? Can you hear Daddy? Jake, pick up the phone, if you can hear me. Nella, if you're still there, don't leave. I don't know what lie John McHill told you, but we're winning this case. Don't go anywhere!"

He waited a few more moments, hoping she'd hear him and pick up the phone, but soon he heard the sharp tone telling him he'd run out of time.

"I ought to beat the hell out of John for this. And Miranda too," he yelled to the empty room around him as he dialed John McHill's number. No answer. He dialed Miranda's number, and John's sleepy voice answered.

"What the hell are you up to?" Sam exploded into the phone.

The drowsiness immediately left John's voice. "Hey, man, what are you talking about?"

"Don't try to bullshit me, John. I got a message from Nella saying you told her I'd lost the case. What's your game, John? Answer me, dammit."

Suddenly Miranda's voice was on the line. Sam had never actually realized how shrill it was.

"Sam, you heard the judge. He said this case wasn't over until he said it was over, and any new evidence will be used. I think the judge might frown on kidnapping, don't you?" She slammed the phone down in Sam's ear.

"Bitch!" Sam exploded at the phone. So that was it. As a last-ditch effort, they'd fed Nella that cock-and-bull story about losing the case so she'd take Jake and run. Now they'd try to convince the judge Nella had kidnapped Jake.

He must act quickly. He picked up the phone and dialed his lawyer's number.

Nella pulled up to her house late Sunday night. Jake was asleep in the back seat.

It had been a long, two-day drive. Nella had tried to make the trip fun, and Jake did enjoy the trip, but Nella was so full of sadness at the thought of losing him that each time he laughed or did something really cute, her heart felt as if it would burst with sorrow, knowing that if Jake's grandparents took him she wouldn't be able to revel in the little things he did anymore. And that she would never even see him again.

After she had Jake tucked in bed for the night, Nella walked through the house and checked everything. It was good to be home, but the house didn't have the same emotional hold on her as it once had. She realized that she didn't care where she lived as long as she could be with the two people she loved most in the world.

What would happen now? Would Sam sell the house to someone else? He had no use for it if he lost Jake.

With a heavy heart, and not knowing what was ahead for them all, Nella finally fell asleep to dark, shadowy dreams of clutching Jake close in her arms and running, running, running.

Chapter 12

Monday morning when Nella awoke, the feeling of doom still hung over her. She couldn't shake the vague, haunting feelings from her dreams the night before.

Would Sam tell anyone she had taken Jake and run? Or would he just let his in-laws waste time going all the way to Kentucky looking for her? How long would it take them to figure out where she was?

The sky was gray and overcast, with the promise of a storm blowing in. Nella felt as if she had to get away from the house. She woke Jake and dressed him, and headed into town.

They ate breakfast at McDonald's. Nella sat outside and let Jake play on the playground equipment. She watched each move he made. Her heart was filled to the brim with love for the little boy.

He seemed completely rested from the trip. He laughed and called to her constantly to watch some new trick he was about to do.

Nella was amazed at how complete her life had become since Sam and Jake were a part of it. Especially Jake. Her future seemed so bleak at the prospect of him not being in it.

"Look, Mommy!" Jake called. Nella looked up to see him standing at the top of the slide, not holding onto anything.

"Jake, honey, sit down. You should never stand up like that. You could fall and hurt yourself very badly," she admonished, as she went and stood under him in case he lost his balance and fell.

Just before Jake sat down, Nella was aware of a bright flash close beside her. After seeing that Jake was safe on the ground, she looked around to see what had caused the flash.

She immediately recognized the sleazeball who had tried to snatch Jake from her once before. He stood leering at her, clutching a 35 mm camera in his grimy hands.

"This'll look real good to the lawyers. You lettin' that little boy get in such a dangerous situation like that," he gloated through tobacco-browned teeth.

Not considering any danger to herself, Nella made a lunge for the camera, but he was too fast for her. He bolted from the playground and ran down the street. Nella knew there was no use in trying to chase him.

"Who was that man, Mommy? Why did he want a picture of me? Do we know him?"

"He's not a nice man, Jake. If you ever see him, you come straight to me, okay?" She didn't want to cause Jake any unnecessary fear, but she had to make him cautious of the man. "And," she continued, "if he ever tries to pick you up, you start calling for help as loudly as you can, okay?"

"Okay, Mommy, I will," Jake promised, and headed back to the slide.

After letting Jake play for a time, Nella took him to a few toy stores and bought him several toys he wanted. After lunch, they went to a Disney movie. By the time the movie was over Jake was getting tired, so she reluctantly headed back to the house, knowing this might be the last day she ever spent with him.

When she pulled into her driveway an unfamiliar car was parked in front of the house. Afraid that the car could belong to someone trying to take Jake, she was about to head back to town when an all-too-familiar figure came around the corner of the house.

"*Nick?*"

Nick, in all of his carefree beauty, looking as if he'd just stepped off a surfboard. Nick, with his bronze skin and his long brown hair blowing in the salty sea breeze. Beautiful, carefree, shallow Nick.

"Hi, baby," he said, approaching her as if a whole year hadn't passed since they'd broken their engagement. "I've missed you so much! Can we try to work things out?"

At that moment Jake, who'd been asleep on the back seat, raised his head and called, "Mommy?"

"What the hell?" Nick stepped back from the embrace he'd been attempting to give Nella. The look of bewilderment on his face was so complete that Nella had to laugh. She leaned into the car and lifted Jake into her arms.

"Nick, this is Jake. He's my stepson."

"Your *whaat?*"

"My stepson. I'm married now."

The wind was blowing harder, and it was beginning to rain. "Come on in, and I'll explain," she said to the open-mouthed man standing in front of her. They'd soon be soaked if they stood outside any longer.

Nella carried Jake and gently placed him on her bed. He was soon back asleep. She made a pot of coffee and proceeded to explain the circumstances of her marriage. She told Nick the incidents that had led to this point. She let him know how much she loved the little boy sleeping on her bed. The only thing she left out was how things had changed between her and Sam.

"Well, why don't you just get a divorce and marry me?" he asked after she'd finished. "And why didn't you call me when your world fell apart like that? We could have worked something out."

"Now, Nick, you and I decided over a year ago that we shouldn't be married. What good would it have done for me to call you?"

"No, *you* decided. I didn't have much choice but to go along with that decision whether I liked it or not. But there's no reason for you to stay married to someone you don't love."

"But I do." Her answer was soft with memories of Sam and the times they'd shared.

"You do what?" Nick asked, not following her line of thought.

"I do love my husband."

"Oh, no! Surely you haven't gotten in that deep."

"'Fraid so," she answered, trying to keep the sad note from her voice.

"Does he love you?" Now Nick sounded truly concerned.

"I don't know." Nella shook her head.

"What a mess! I wish now I would've just insisted you marry me, and you would never have had to go through all this."

"Nick, that's a sweet thought, but you and I would probably already be divorced if we'd married a year ago. We have a great relationship. We can talk and laugh and enjoy each other's company, but our values and goals in life are totally different. It would just never work. We established that a year ago."

Her reasoning fell on unhearing ears.

"We could both work on our differences. We could both change a little, and come to a compromise."

"Nick, I've had a really bad few days. I'm real tired. I need to go to bed and rest. Could you please leave now?" Nella saw no reason to continue their conversation.

"Are you really going to send me out into that storm? Listen to the wind blowing. And those waves sound like they're landing on the patio outside."

Nella had been aware of the building storm outside, so she reluctantly gave in. "Okay, you can spend the night, but in the morning you have to be on your way, okay? I've got too much to deal with right now to even consider what might or might not could be between you and me." She didn't want to hurt him anymore, but because of her love for Sam she could never consider trying to get back into a relationship with Nick.

"Thanks, I'll sack out here on the couch, and in the morning I'll leave. But as soon as this thing with the kid blows over, I'm coming back and we're going to try to work things out."

Nella didn't try to argue with him. At this point she didn't have the strength. Wearily, she went to bed to spend another restless night.

The next morning, she came dully awake to a fierce pounding on her front door. Fear shot through her like a bolt of lightning. Were they already here to take Jake from her? Surely they wouldn't have found her this soon. Then she remembered Sleazeball with his camera. He probably called yesterday as soon as he'd found she was back in town.

By the time she managed to get her robe on, the pounding had stopped. And so did her heart when she came through her bedroom door and surveyed the picture before her.

Jake sat at the kitchen table eating a bowl of cereal. Nick had opened the door, wearing nothing but a pair of jogging shorts that were wrinkled from having been slept in. His hair was in total disarray and it was obvious to the onlookers at the door that he had spent the night.

Nella knew her appearance wasn't any better. In her haste to see who was banging her door down, she had barely pulled the robe around herself. Her hair looked ten times worse than Nick's.

The first eyes that she looked into were Sam's.

Then Sheriff Dansby stepped into the room.

"Nella, what the hell is going on? These people have filed kidnapping charges against you. I've got to arrest you and take you in for questioning."

"Questioning be damned! I want her put away for a long time!" The person speaking was a woman, but with different clothing could easily have passed as a man. Nella knew immediately that she was looking at Sam's former mother-in-law.

"Now, easy, Hon," chirped a small man standing slightly behind the woman speaking. It was obvious who called the shots here.

"Shut up, Josh. I want this bitch punished for all she's put my grandbaby through," she said coldly. She went over to Jake and tried to hug him, but he jumped down from his chair and ran to Nella.

Jake's eyes were full of fear, and Nella reached down and lifted him in her arms. He wrapped his arms around her neck and buried his face in her hair, as if to hide from the ugly scene taking place in front of him.

"Quiet!" Nella recognized the fury in Sam's voice. "I want everyone out of this house right now! I need a few words with my wife."

Just then a flash from a camera went off. A reporter had managed to squeeze through the door. Sam snatched the camera from the reporter and threw it out the door, pushing the man out with it.

Finally the room was cleared of everyone except Sam, Nella, and Jake.

Sam reached for Jake and held him tightly. Nella wanted to feel those strong arms close around her, but Sam made no attempt to draw her to him. Instead he asked, "Who's the beach bum?"

"Nick."

"The old fiancé?"

"Yes."

"What's he doing here?" Sam's voice was full of unasked questions that wanted answers.

"He came over last night to try to get me to reconcile with him. The storm caught him, so I agreed to let him spend the night. As you can see, he slept on the couch."

The couch cushions were mussed and there was a sheet and pillow on the couch.

"I believe you, Nella," Sam reassured her, "but you can't begin to imagine what the press will do with this, and how it'll hurt our case." The stress from the past couple of weeks had caused Sam's face to look drawn and haggard.

"But we lost. That's what John McHill said on the phone. And I just wanted to give you a little more time. Didn't you get my message?"

"Yes, I got your message. You were set up, Nella. John and Miranda were trying to get you to do exactly what you did."

"Set up?" Nella's voice was weak with disbelief that she had done more harm than good by leaving Kentucky with Jake.

"When John made that call to you, they had my line tapped. When you called me, they taped it and took it straight to the lawyers."

"That's enough time!" someone yelled from outside the door.

"You'd better get dressed," Sam told Nella. "Don't worry, I'm not finished. We haven't lost yet."

In a stupor, Nella showered and dressed. What lay ahead of her? Would she actually go to jail for kidnapping? Could they do that to her? As if sleepwalking, she went back and joined Sam and Jake in the living room.

Sam led Nella through the crowd that had gathered in front of her house. Reporters stuck microphones in her face, asking questions she didn't even hear, as cameras flashed all around them. There were two local TV camera crews already there.

Sam handed Jake to Nella so she could say good-bye to him. His small arms clamped tightly around her neck, and she held him as close to her as she could. They were both weeping when Sam finally had to pry Jake from her arms.

Sam leaned over and kissed Nella softly on the lips before she sat down in the front seat with Sheriff Dansby.

"Thank you for trying to help," he whispered, before closing the door.

As the car pulled from the driveway, the only sounds were the crunching of the tires on the gravel and Jake calling, "Don't take my mommy, don't take my mommy! I want my mommy!"

"Sometimes I hate my job," Harmon Dansby muttered as the sheriff's car sped toward town and Nella sat crying into her hands, awaiting an uncertain future.

The metal clanking of the cell doors closing was the most horrifying sound Nella had ever heard.

"Nella, girl, I'm so sorry to have to do this. But I know you won't be in here long. I know you aren't a kidnapper." Sheriff Dansby was trying to console her, but Nella was in a state of shock he couldn't penetrate. Finally he said, "Now you remember what you told me about being a survivor! You've got to survive, Nella. You've got to do it for your dad's sake, and for your own."

Getting no response from her, the sheriff shrugged tiredly and left the room.

All day, lawyers from both sides questioned Nella. By evening she was so weary and exhausted she could barely move. But she didn't sleep at all that night. She didn't even lie down. She just sat on the hard bunk and stared into the darkness, reliving each moment of her life since she'd met and married Sam and become a mother to Jake.

Even when breakfast was brought in the next morning, she made no attempt to eat, but continued to sit and reminisce. She didn't regret becoming a part of Sam and Jake's life. Her life had been complete for a few months. Totally and fully complete. That's more than some people ever had. She would take those few months and revel in them for the rest of her life.

Sam would surely want a divorce now. He'd be brokenhearted at losing Jake, and would probably hate her for the part she'd played in his loss.

It tore Nella apart to know she'd played a major role in causing Sam and Jake to be separated. If she'd only stayed in Kentucky. If she'd just told Nick he couldn't spend the night at her house. So many ifs. Sam and Jake would have been better off if they'd never met her!

"Nella?" Sheriff Dansby's voice preceded him. "You can go now. The kidnapping charges have been dropped. I knew you couldn't be guilty of such a thing."

Nella glanced at her watch. Eleven a.m. "What do you mean, Harmon? Why have the charges been dropped?" Too numb from her ordeal to think, reality didn't sink in for a few moments.

"After the lawyers questioned you yesterday, and after the press covered yours and Jake's tearful parting, the lawyers decided they didn't have a case that would stand up. That little boy obviously adores you. It was really heartbreaking to watch him on TV last night. The whole county is in a turmoil about it. The public wants to put the boy's grandparents in jail for putting him through this kind of ordeal."

By now Nella was at the desk collecting her personal items. She was afraid to ask the next question. "Have you heard from Sam?"

"No, honey. I haven't heard a thing. But come on, I'll take you home. I have to go out that way on a domestic call."

Nella knew he was just using that as an excuse to take her home. Everyone in her community had been married for years with no problems at all, as far as Nella had ever heard.

When he dropped her off at her house, Nella thanked him, and watched as he drove away. There was no sign of Sam's car. She wondered where he was.

She didn't go into the house. She headed down the steps to the beach, hoping the lapping waves would lull her frayed senses and make her feel better. Although at this point, she wondered if that would ever be possible again.

She didn't know how far she walked, but weariness from everything she'd been through eventually overtook her, so she headed back toward her house. Maybe if she ate some hot soup, she'd be able to lie down and sleep a little. If she could just sleep and relax she'd be in a better state of mind to try to figure out what she was going to do next.

She was approaching the steps that led up to her house when the writing in the sand caught her eyes.

"Jake" was written in huge letters. An arrow pointed toward the steps.

Excitement shot through her, expunging all the weariness. She bounded up the steps, and there in her lounge chair lay Sam with Jake lying on his stomach. It was an exact replay of their first meeting, except Sam and Jake were not asleep.

"Surprise!" they called in unison.

Nella slumped into the closest chair. Tears rolled freely down her face.

"Don't cry, Mommy." Jake ran to her and took her face in his hands. "I missed you last night. Where were you? Daddy and I were here, but you never came home."

Nella looked at Sam with a question in her eyes.

"After Dansby hauled you away, I persuaded the lawyers that Jake needed the comfort of being in a familiar surrounding after all he'd just been through. So they decided to wait until today to turn him over to his grandparents."

"Oh, no, don't tell me I'm going to have to go through losing him all over again!" Nella was distraught at the thought of having Jake pulled from her arms again.

"No. After the lawyers finished questioning you, and after the story made such a splash on the news last night, the judge decided this morning that Jake should remain with his parents."

"His parents?" Nella felt warmth slowly engulfing her.

"Yes, Mommy, my parents," Jake explained, as if talking to a child much younger than himself. "You know, you and Daddy."

"So you have full custody now?" Nella asked, still not quite able to believe their ordeal was over.

"Total," he assured her. "Jake's grandparents can see him if and when I allow it, but I must always be present when they're with him. That's their punishment for trying to run a scam on the courts. So Jake is in my custody now and forever."

"No matter what happens?" she asked, almost afraid of the answer.

"No matter what happens." Sam's eyes were beginning to crinkle around the edges as he subdued a smile. He knew where Nella was going with this line of questioning.

But Nella was serious, needing, but afraid of hearing, the answer to her next question. "Then that means you don't have to have me in the picture as a stabilizing part of Jake's life anymore. Where does that leave me? Where does that leave us?" She literally held her breath, waiting for Sam's answer.

"Well," his voice was calm. How could he be so calm at a time like this? "I'm not sure, but if you love me half as much as I love you, it seems to leave us with a future packed full of love for each other and our children."

Nella couldn't move. She could only look into those beloved golden brown eyes and try to make herself believe what she'd just heard.

"And if you keep looking at me like that, we might just have to start adding those other children right now." Sam got up from his chair and pulled Nella to her feet.

She was still in a daze as Sam lowered his lips to claim hers.

After a long, gentle kiss, he raised his head. His voice was husky with emotion as he said, "I love you, Nella. I love everything about you. The biggest mistake I ever made was thinking I would never be attracted to you. I think even then, I was trying to convince myself. Please say you love me, and that you'll stay married to me."

"I do love you, Sam. I think I've loved you from the beginning. I tried to not like you at all because of your rotten attitude, but the harder I tried not to like you, the more I loved you. There's nothing I want more than to stay married to you — if that's what you really want. But," she warned, "make sure its what you want, because once you make that commitment, you're never going to get rid of me."

"I'm getting hungry, people."

The small voice reminded them that Jake was still there. They broke into laughter at his indignant declaration.

"Daddy, you said we could go get a hambooger as soon as Nella got finished with her walk."

"So you were here all along?" Nella asked Sam. "Where's the car? I didn't see anyone when Harmon dropped me off."

"I parked it down the beach behind a sand dune. In fact, I parked it in the same place I hid it from you the day you found Jake alone on the beach." He knew he had to tell her the truth about their first meeting. He couldn't let her keep thinking he'd actually lost Jake that day.

"You did *what?*" Nella didn't believe what she'd just heard.

"Now, Nella, don't get angry. I didn't really lose Jake that day. I kind of set you up to find him. I wanted to see how you'd respond to an emergency. I know it probably wasn't the best way to do things, but it was the first thing I thought about, and I was kind of in a hurry to get acquainted with you. I already knew you were the woman I wanted to take care of my son."

"How did you know that? Had you been watching me?" Nella was feeling real anger at Sam for the first time since she'd known him. She knew her eyes reflected that anger.

"I'd spent a couple of weeks making inquiries about you. The first time I saw you was in a grocery store talking to a lady and her baby. I liked the way you responded to the baby, so I started asking questions. Lady, you sure have a fine reputation in these here parts." Sam tried to lighten the mood. He could tell Nella was angry at having been deceived about their first meeting. "And, let me add, your eyes are even more beautiful when you're angry than they usually are."

"Don't try to joke your way out of this, Sam du Cannon!" But even as Nella scolded him, she could feel her anger slipping away. "I shouldn't be surprised. You are the most persistent man I've ever known. I'll try to forgive you, but it's going to take a long, long time." Now she was the one teasing.

Sam pulled her to him once again, and held her close. "I've missed you so much. I can't wait to make love to you again."

"I really need a hambooger!" Jake was beginning to grow impatient.

"I'll get the car," Sam suggested, "and we'll go somewhere and feed this hungry kid. It's been a while since he had breakfast."

"But Sam, I'm so grimy from spending the night in — "

Sam's hand was clamped lightly over her mouth before she said the word "jail."

"Jake doesn't know," Sam whispered. "Besides, we'll just go to some small place where there aren't a lot of people. Come on, you look wonderful to me, just like you are."

While Sam went for the car, Nella freshened her makeup and combed her hair. Soon they were heading into town. Sam parked the car in front of the small restaurant where he'd first asked her to marry him.

When they went in he whispered something to the hostess who seated them, and she hurried away.

"Sam, what are you up to?"

"Just asking for 'our' table," he reassured her.

After a short wait, the hostess came back and escorted them to the booth where they had sat on that first day. Sam made sure Nella was seated, then unexpectedly dropped to one knee. He took both of Nella's hands in his, and then nodded to the hostess.

"Okay, Sally."

Sally gave a signal, and suddenly people surrounded them. A couple of people held TV cameras.

Once everyone had settled down, Sam looked into Nella's astonished eyes and said, "Nella, the first time we came here, I asked you to marry me because I needed a mother for Jake. This time, I'm asking you to stay married to me because I love you totally, and want to spend the rest of my life with you. I want you to be the mother of my child, Jake, and I want you to be the mother of any other children we may be blessed with. Will you spend your life with me, Nella?"

"Yes," was the only word Nella could get her voice to produce.

Sam rose and kissed Nella long and hard, until the congratulations and backslapping began.

The story made the Charleston news that night, and the society section of the paper the next day. The story concluded by saying the family would spend winters at their Kentucky home, and summers at their South Carolina beach home.

About the Author

Pat Ballard lives in Nashville, TN. She writes motivational romance novels with Big Beautiful Heroines to show that plus-size women can be just as sexy, romantic, and exciting as their slim sisters.

Visit Pat at www.patballard.com.

Check out other books by Pat — and more — at the Pearlsong Press website at www.pearlsong.com.